## ABOUT THE AUTHOR

Chris started creating stories not long after she mastered joined-up writing, somewhat to the bemusement of her parents and her English teachers. But she received plenty of encouragement. Her dad gave her an already old Everest typewriter when she was ten, and it was probably the best gift she'd ever received— until the inventions of the home computer and the World-Wide Web.

Chris's reading and writing interests range from historical, mystery, and paranormal, to science fiction and fantasy, mostly in the male/male. She also writes male/female novels in the name of Chris Power. She refuses to be pigeon-holed and intends to uphold the long and honourable tradition of the Eccentric Brit to the best of her ability. In her spare time [hah!] she embroiders, quilts and knits. In the past she worked for her local Constabulary as a behind-the-scenes civilian for over twenty years, has been a part-time and unpaid amateur archaeologist, and a 15th century re-enactor.

She currently lives in a small and ancient city in the southwest of the United Kingdom, sharing her usually chaotic home with an extended family, two large dogs, an Australian Bearded Dragon, and sundry goldfish.

Her websites are:
http://chrisquinton.com and http://chrispower.me.uk

Blog:
chris-quinton.livejournal.com

Facebook:
http://tinyurl.com/67o4mrm

# GAME ON,
# GAME OVER

## CHRIS QUINTON

Published by Silver Publishing
Publisher of Erotic Romance

# SILVERPUBLISHING

ISBN 978-1-61495-364-7

Game On, Game Over

Copyright © 2011 by Chris Quinton
Editor: Lisa Manuel
Cover Artist: Reese Dante

Visit Silver Publishing at https://spsilverpublishing.com

# NOTE FROM THE PUBLISHER

Dear Reader,

Thank you for your purchase of this title. The authors and staff of Silver Publishing hope you enjoy this read and that we will have a long and happy association together.

Please remember that the only money authors make from writing comes from the sales of their books. If you like their work, spread the word and tell others about the books, but please refrain from copying this book in any form. Authors depend on sales and sales only to support their families.

If you see "free shares" offered or cut-rate sales on pirate sites of this title, you can report the offending entry to copyright@spsilverpublishing.com

Thank you for not pirating our titles.

Lodewyk Deysel
Publisher
Silver Publishing
http://www.spsilverpublishing.com

## DEDICATION:

To all my friends who support, nag,
commiserate and cheer me on -
Thank you. Writing wouldn't be quite so much
fun without you all.

# TRADEMARKS ACKNOWLEDGEMENT

PART ONE - GAME ON

## CHAPTER ONE

"The first meeting is close to being set up," Daryush said as the battered 4X4 jolted from rut to rut. "Gulab Turi is oldest among the tribal leaders. He has the most influence as well and if anyone can unite most of the tribes and turn them against the Taliban, it's him. I've laid some of the groundwork, but he wants to horse-trade for his cooperation. Get him on your side and he'll introduce you to the other leaders and make sure they fall into line." He wrestled the clutch to a lower gear and they lurched up the hill, more or less following the line of the track.

"How reluctant is Gulab?" John braced his knees against the dashboard and prayed he wouldn't pop his kneecaps.

Daryush's teeth gleamed in the black tangle of his beard. Despite some streaks of gray in his rough-cut hair and the deep lines at the corners of his eyes, his features were those of a man in his early thirties, a handful of years younger than John. "Not very. He doesn't want anyone telling him how to run his territory. Not the government over in Dushanbe, not the UN, the USA, Russia, or the fucking Taliban."

They were talking in Daryush's native Tajik, a language John spoke fluently, as he did Uzbek, Farsi, Russian, and assorted others both ancient and modern. His ability with the languages and dialects of Central Asia was one of the reasons why he'd been recruited straight out of Oxford by MI6. His photographic memory also proved an asset.

Once more he took up his usual role of negotiator, the intermediary between prospective allies, and he looked forward to both aspects of his current assignment, the overt and the covert. *The Great Game*, as immortalized by Rudyard Kipling, was alive and well and going strong. Only the protagonists changed.

Daryush Akramov and his brother Azad had worked for MI6 before, as 'trusted associates' rather than agents, and John certainly trusted both of them. They'd all been part of a particularly nasty mission in Northern Afghanistan six years ago. As much by luck as judgment, John had hauled them out of a potentially fatal situation. The brothers didn't forget.

"Any possible complications?" he asked the Tajik, wincing as the vehicle bucked over a series of deep potholes.

"Shaheen Jalil." Daryush waved his hand in a vaguely eastern direction. "He's in bed with the Taliban, but he's two days of bad roads from the Afghan border, not close enough to give them much active support. He's been putting pressure on the other leaders between him and the Afghans: Gulab, Mazdak Rudaki, and Jahandar Rakhmon. Mazdak is wobbling."

"And if Shaheen is removed from the equation?"

"His eldest son takes over. Ardshir is even more of a hardliner. He's a fanatic."

John frowned. The Tajik government must be well aware of the inherent instability of the area, yet they'd gone ahead and approved an international archaeological dig. Contacts in Dushanbe surmised the Tajik government was attempting to prove to the world they held total control over the region. So far, three months into the actual dirt archaeology, all was calm, but the situation could so quickly end in tragedy and blood.

"Okay," he said. "Last resort, we'll take them both out if we have to. Until then, we'll work around them."

"You're the boss," Daryush said easily.

"There is another problem. American, this time."

"Damn. At the dig?" For the last three months, Daryush and his brother had been part of the small army ferrying in supplies, water, and the occasional visitor from Khorog and the much closer Ishkoshim, one of their jobs as the local jacks-of-all-trades.

"Not yet. Brent Babcock. He's a freelance journalist. He's been following some of the old Silk Roads, gathering material for a book, he says. Started out at Tashkurgan on the Chinese border, got as far as the Hanis Guesthouse in Ishkoshim two days ago. He's been asking questions about the Road and its offshoots. I'm driving him and his cameraman out to the dig in a couple of days. He's also asking about the political situation, border troubles, gems and drugs, and gunrunning."

"Bugger." Inquisitive Americans were

difficult to get rid of, doubly so when they were journalists. The name sounded familiar as well. First chance he got, John would check him out.

"Is he getting any answers?"

"Probably. He's throwing a lot of money around."

"Idiot. He's going to end up on the wrong end of a ransom deal if he isn't careful."

"Azad is keeping an eye on them," Daryush assured him, grinning again. Being the local odd-job men gave the brothers a great deal of useful leeway. No one ever seemed to question what they were doing and with whom they spent time. Which suited MI6 and John very well.

The excavation site lay in the mouth of a shallow valley stretching north-south, opening onto a wider east-west valley where a Silk Road ran in the 11th century. A caravanserai once stood there, but a long-ago earthquake partially destroyed the buildings, cracked the underground water cisterns, and changed the course of the spring. The loss of the water struck the death knell for the caravanserai, and it was never rebuilt. Rerouting of the Silk Road some miles south, closer to the Panj River, left the ruins largely untouched, if not entirely forgotten. A few centuries later another quake brought down the hillside, partially burying the site.

The museum in Tajikistan's capital city, Dushanbe, didn't have the funds or resources to excavate on its own, but international deals had been made and the dig was up and running with the assistance of postgraduate students and experts from three countries as well as Dushanbe University.

At John's request, Daryush stopped on the crest of the last rise, giving him a chance to look down on the excavations. Fortunately for the archaeologists, the site was far enough from Ishkoshim and the other outlying villages for it to have escaped being completely robbed out for building stone. Historically, only a few local farmers had used it as a quarry. Most of the outer walls of the caravanserai were visible. Originally the complex had probably been a large rectangle built of cream-colored stone, the northern section remained buried under ancient rock falls. Some exposed walls still stood several meters high, as did the ruined gate towers.

Neat trenches cut through the rubble of ages, and small figures swarmed about. Even from a distance, John could appreciate their purposefulness. On the near side of the site, a spoil heap grew, made of earth dug out of the trenches. It was regularly added to by archaeologists carrying buckets or pushing wheelbarrows. Close by, a team industriously sifted soil from the mound through fine-meshed sieves, separating dirt from tiny fragments; the samples for analysis would give them information on climate and vegetation. Their efforts were generating the growth of a second mound.

On the far side of the complex, the land rose again. There, on a small plateau, sat the encampment, a neatly laid out tent village with a central space for socializing and one very large tent which was probably the mess. One solid building stood out among the bright fabrics: a long, low prefabricated structure John guessed would house the finds, workrooms, and the Site Directors' offices. A range of portable toilets and washing facilities fed by a couple of tankers stood off to one side, a few of them partitioned from the others by a high screen.

Out of sight and an hour away to the

south, ran the Panj River and the Afghanistan border. Once again, John doubted the sanity of the Dushanbe government and the participating universities.

"Okay?" Daryush asked but didn't wait for an answer. Instead he slammed the truck into gear and stamped on the accelerator, heading down the hill in a hail of scattered stones, the engine bellowing like an enraged bull.

A welcoming committee of two waited for John: Professor Mike Preston, Site Director, and Doctor Nikki Hanley, the Assistant Director John would be replacing. He was greeted with friendly smiles and hand shakes, Nikki's being a double hand-clasp as if he was an old friend. She almost vibrated with suppressed excitement; a top-level post awaited her back in the UK with the newly formed Mercia Archaeological Trust. Because MI6 needed a way to slide John into the area for the two or three months his negotiations might take, she had been headhunted to make way for him.

A small part of John envied her. He enjoyed his job, was good at it, and he cheerfully admitted to being an adrenaline addict. But at the same time, he acknowledged a deep-buried longing for a more academic career. *Maybe one day...* Before MI6, he'd been Aidan Whittaker, graduating with honors from Oxford. With a view to a future where he would no longer be an agent, John, as Aidan, maintained a literary presence by submitting the occasional article to various highbrow magazines. The latest one dealt with translations of and background history behind some newly discovered letters from Cesare Borgia, and was due out any day. But most of the time he was John Jones, the holder of two not-entirely fake doctorates gained by Aidan Whittaker: one in

Archaeology and the other in Ancient Languages and Literature. The Jones identity had served him and MI6 well for some fourteen years so far, but he didn't often get the chance to use his expertise in an archaeological setting.

"You made good time," Mike said. He was tall, well over six feet, and as bulky as a graying, late-middle-aged bear. "We thought we'd have to wait quite a while for a replacement to show up. It's good to have you aboard."

"It's good to be here," John answered. "I'd just finished a translation job in Budapest when the agency contacted me. I grabbed at this so fast hands might have been in danger."

Mike laughed. "Yes, I read your application with a lot of interest, and we could well have some good stuff in store for you. We've found some inscriptions, but we've also come across a cache of religious scrolls and letter tablets from the tenth and eleventh centuries, and some of them seem to be Greek as well as Persian."

"Fantastic!" John did not have to fake his passion.

Mike slapped him on the shoulder. "Come on," he said. "We'll give you the grand tour. There are twenty postgraduate students from four universities," he continued. "Dushanbe, Manhattan, Bristol, and Rome. We have three lecturers doubling up as specialists. Anahita Kamyarova is pottery and ceramics, and she's been covering inscriptions as well, though it isn't really her forte. Rosie Lane is bones and preservation, and Yves Bonneau covers coins and metalwork. You and your language knowledge will be a welcome fourth. Rosie and Yves are both trained first aiders, by the way.

"The students get some time off to go

into Ishkoshim on Saturdays for the market, but only in groups. No solo trips. My grasp of Russian is very basic, but we make sure each group has at least one Russian speaker with them. That's the only chaperoning we do. All of them are over twenty-one, and we can't be nursemaids." He broke off with a shrug. "But they're a pretty good bunch and the girls are sensible about what they wear, here as well as in the village. Every now and then some of the postgrads hit a series of relationship crises and they play Musical Beds, but there've been no major traumas. The casualties usually cry on Anahita's or Rosie's shoulders, and it all blows over. There've been no problems at all with the locals, though every so often a squad of soldiers turns up to check on us. No need to worry. They haven't given us any trouble so far."

Archaeologists have their own priorities,

and John's introductory tour started with the excavations and meeting most of the students and lecturers. John had already noted Nikki wore loosely fitting trousers and a long-sleeved tunic, her hair covered by a headscarf. The other two female lecturers and four postgraduates wore similar outfits, sensible concessions to local religious sensitivities.

Then Mike showed him the finds, the preservation unit, and the two offices, all in the building John had seen from the rise. Nikki's office was now his. She talked nonstop, her enthusiasm and expertise clearly evident. She would be a hard act to follow.

"The generators are reasonably efficient," Mike told him. "We usually have enough power for the computers, but we do the initial recording and report writing the old-fashioned way. Be warned, though. Internet and mobile phone reception can be pretty erratic."

"No problem." John smiled. His own encrypted, six-ways-to-Sunday satellite phone, courtesy of MI6, was for emergencies only. His normal reporting link was via his mobile phone to Maria Jaeger of BHARA, the Bickerstall Historical & Archaeological Resources Agency; Maria doubled as his legitimate agent and frontline contact with MI6.

"One of your duties as Assistant Director will be liaising with the locals," Nikki said. "I would have liked to take you around and introduce you myself, but I have to go back with Daryush after lunch. He knows them all, though, and he's said he doesn't mind doing the honors. Everyone out there speaks Russian, more or less, and—you do, too, don't you?" she asked anxiously.

"Yes," he assured her. "I'm fluent. Daryush already tested me on it during the drive here."

"Oh, good. He's been a godsend, really," she continued, "even if he does talk the hind leg off a donkey." John suppressed a grin and Mike chuckled. "There are a few outlying sites in need of exploration, but I didn't get around to following them up. They're all in my notes." She tapped a bulging file sitting beside the laptop computer. "There's power to the lecturers' tents, so you can take this back there if you want to work in peace and quiet. Oh, you're taking over my tent as well. It's a perk of being a lecturer, having your own space. Everyone else is doubled up."

"Okay, that's about it," Mike said cheerfully. "We'll leave you to get your kit unpacked. Your tent is the blue one with the green flag outside. Lunch will be in half an hour, dinner at six tonight, and there's a buffet breakfast at eight. The caterers show up every morning and stay until after dinner in the evening. The food is pretty good, mostly local cuisine, but no one's complained so far."

The mess tent, the large white pavilion, had already been pointed out, and John's stomach reminded him his breakfast had happened far too early. "Great," he said. "I'll see you both over there."

The comfortably large dome tent John inherited was tall enough for him to stand up in. The sleeping area consisted of a large separate compartment through a zippered door, where a narrow camp bed with a pallet and a stack of blankets awaited his sleeping bag. The nights could get cold, he knew. The spacious living area held a canvas chair, a folding table, some storage racks, and generator-fed power sources for the light and his laptop. A faint aroma of flowery vanilla lingered in the still air, a fast-fading echo of Nikki's erstwhile presence.

Used to traveling light, it didn't take John long to make himself at home. The tent would be more comfortable than some hotels he'd stayed in recently. He sent a short text to Maria reporting his arrival at the site, then headed for the mess tent, his stomach growling its impatience. So far the overt mission was progressing smoothly. He hoped the covert side would be as problem-free, but that seemed as likely as the Taliban declaring peace and love for all things Western.

By the third day John was fully integrated into the closed society of the archaeological site and the personnel working on it. They were a gregarious bunch, passionate about what they were doing, but capable of amusement at their own expense. All the lecturers were over forty years old, and their relationships with the much younger students were governed by mutual respect and liking. The Tajik locals running the catering, laundry, and site security were friendly, proud of their past, and appreciative of the interest their culture and history fired in foreigners. All in all, the whole, mismatched conglomerate worked together with cheerful tolerance and good humor. But the third day also brought Brent Babcock.

John was with Anahita in her trench, an exploratory cut along an inside wall of the caravanserai where some scroll ends and clay tablets had already been found. She was speculating optimistically about further finds when a voice laden with a harsh New York twang cut through her lightly accented English like a blunt saw. John peered over the edge of the trench and saw a man in his late forties, short, stocky, with thinning hair in a buzz cut, and the face of a pugnacious leprechaun. He was talking animatedly with Mike, hands waving to emphasize his points.

"Who the hell?" John muttered. But he'd lingered aboveground too long. Mike gestured to him—desperately, if he was any judge—and reluctantly he climbed out of the trench.

"John, this is Brent Babcock," Mike said as soon as he joined the two men. Babcock barely topped John's shoulder and John was a lean six feet tall. Mike's solid six-five dwarfed them both. "Mr Babcock, Doctor John Jones, my Assistant Director. John, Mr Babcock's a reporter—"

"Journalist," Babcock interrupted, sticking out his hand. John took it. "Hi. I'm writing a series of articles on the Silk Roads, and gathering material for a book." Their handshake was brief, Babcock's grip strong to the point of discomfort. John managed to resist the impulse to tighten his own grip in response to the power play.

"You've chosen a fascinating subject," he said mildly.

"Yeah, I know. This was the Lost Road of Ishkoshim, right?" The capital letters were obvious, the title of the book and a TV documentary probably already scripted in the man's mind.

"Um, it wasn't actually lost," Mike said. "This spur of it was simply abandoned after the quake in the eleventh century. The spring and cisterns were—"

"Yeah, I get it. Like I said before I want to hear your take on it, some of the background history to the dig. Take some photos as well."

Mike frowned thoughtfully. "I'll have to clear it with the higher-ups first," he answered. "But I don't expect it'll be much of a problem. We're not exactly rewriting the history books here, and though the finds have been interesting, it's not in the same category as Tutankhamun's tomb. I'll contact them and let you know."

"Okay. I'm not on a tight schedule. I can afford to spend some time on this. I got a photographer in tow. I'd like him to have a look around, get an impression of the site while you're getting the go-ahead from your bosses." As if the result was a foregone conclusion.

"I don't see a problem," Mike said. "On the strict understanding no pictures are taken until sanctioned, and while either of you are on site, you're accompanied by one of my people at all times."

"I can live with that. You got a deal, Mike." Babcock's hand shot out again. "Call me Brent."

"I'll leave you with Doctor Jones," Mike said, shaking his hand and wincing slightly. His brief sidelong glance at John was apologetic. "He'll be your liaison."

It wasn't what John wanted to hear. But it was a logical choice. Liaising was part of his job description as far as the site was concerned, but if the man and his photographer were going to be underfoot for an unspecified period of time, they might adversely affect his covert mission. While a journalist wouldn't be as easily removed from the scene as an archaeologist, it was certainly doable—and would be done if or when necessary.

Babcock talked at John for over half an hour, and it was as well John was skilled in keeping his thoughts and emotions from showing on his features. His usual friendly mask remained unshaken despite the journalist's belligerent arrogance, but there was no doubt Babcock was good at what he did. His grasp of the history and trade dynamics of the Roads was excellent. The man was intelligent and articulate—borderline     too     articulate—and thoroughly unlikeable.

That night John lulled himself to sleep imagining various devious and intricate plans for the permanent removal of Brent Babcock.

# CHAPTER TWO

The previous day, Babcock had arranged to return to the site at noon, potentially throwing a wrench into John's carefully planned day right from the start. John's initial objective was to visit a backcountry farmer who found some glazed tiles while digging out the foundations for a wall. The unearthed tiles weren't the main reason for the expedition. Gulab Turi would be at a supporter's house in the area, and through a chain of contacts, Gulab had agreed to a meeting. The tribal leader's good will was essential in brokering the deal to unite the tribes against the local Taliban sympathizers. Their meeting could not be postponed, nor could John have a journalist tagging along. It was impossible to explain the situation to Mike, so he did the only thing he could—leave before breakfast after promising Mike he'd be back in time to deal with Babcock. He wouldn't, of course, but ruffled feathers could be smoothed afterwards. Gulab and the deal he hoped to eventually cement were far more important.

Azad ferried John to his first destination, a small oasis of green on each side of a narrow river, half an hour from the excavations. Some fields, a handful of fruit trees, and a fairly substantial house hinted the farmer and his family were doing well in the otherwise virtually barren land. Half an hour's work with his trowel told John the tiles were very similar to the ones turning up at the dig. They'd probably been robbed from the ruins of the caravanserai many years ago, and reused as flooring for a long-vanished house. The shallow footings remained, but they had been covered over when the area was built up and leveled by the current owner's grandfather. John happily accepted the invitation to share their midday meal, and spent another pleasant hour with the man and his family over cups of green tea, communal bowls of palav, and flatbreads. Then Azad drove him east and north, traveling farther into the mountains.

The meeting with Gulab went well, paving the way for more formal discussions—aka wheeling and dealing—with the other leaders. A man of cold practicalities and common sense gained in more than sixty years of hard living, Gulab proved to be very aware of the risks he was taking, and equally conscious they needed to be taken for the good of his people. It helped, too, that he and John found a certain rapport. So much so, Gulab gave him a warning.

"Mazdak Rudaki," Gulab said as they prepared to go their separate ways. "He begins to play with fire. This may well aid us, since he offends those more powerful than he. But at the same time, he seeks to gain allies who would tip the balance their way. It may well happen that I will have to act. Not you, Doctor John Jones. *I*."

In other words, keep your head down and let me deal with this my way. John nodded. "I understand," he said respectfully. He was more than glad to comply. The Western powers did not want to be seen so closely engaged in local unrest. John's own mission did not involve assassinations or conflicts, just bargaining.

Gulab inclined his head. "I'll keep in touch with you through the Akramov brothers and arrange another meeting when I have news. Take coffee with me before you leave, Doctor Jones."

John finally returned to the caravanserai site in the late afternoon. Mike strode toward them, anger flags flying, as the truck came to a halt. Azad, a younger, skinnier version of Daryush, dived out of the cab, full of profuse apologies in a flood of Russian so swift and idiosyncratic Mike almost certainly couldn't follow him.

"That motherless truck! It broke down!" Azad babbled, waving an already prepared blown gasket under the startled director's nose as proof. "I always carry spare parts because, Allah be praised, you never know, but it took me far longer to fix than I thought and there was no signal for Doctor Jones's cell so he couldn't tell you—"

Mike held up his hands. "Slow down! It's all right, just cool off. John, can you get over to Anahita's trench? She's got another cache of scrolls, by the look of it."

"Will do," he said quickly. "Um, sorry about Babcock, but we—"

"It could have been worse." Mike

interrupted with a shrug. "The man is a pain in the arse but he didn't hang around long. Did say he'd be back later on this afternoon, though, so don't disappear again. Do we have another site, by the way?"

John shook his head. "No, not this time. I'll write up my report and let you have it."

"Thanks. It's just as well the site's a nonstarter. God knows we have enough on our plate with what we have here. I never expected the first lot of scrolls, let alone the new ones. The preservation team doesn't know whether to celebrate or tear their hair out."

John knew exactly how Rosie and her two trainee assistants felt. The contents of the writing tablets and scrolls sometimes pulled strongly, threatening to distract him from his mission in ways he hadn't experienced in a very long time. "I better get over there and see what Anahita's got," he said, and jogged across the site to the trench dug across one of the inner walls.

At first John couldn't concentrate on Anahita's find, the meeting with Gulab Turi uppermost in his mind. But gradually the square recess in the partially excavated wall caught and held his attention. The trench had been laid down to explore the foundations of a house built against the wall dividing the caravanserai into two, probably equal, parts. The second courtyard and its buildings lay almost completely buried by fallen masonry and landslides. Luckily for the archaeologists, the centuries had compacted the latter to a stable mass.

Anahita knelt at the far end of the trench, where an inner wall abutted with the more substantial outer wall.

"I'm nowhere near floor level yet," she

said excitedly as he crouched beside her. "Another three feet to go, maybe. But look at this; I think I have the beginnings of a row of small compartments built against the back wall. The first one is packed with rubble, but this one has been closed off by these roof tiles and there's space behind it." By this time she forgot her English and gabbled in Russian. "I shone a torch inside and there are scrolls! Look!" She snatched a pen-torch out of her pocket and thrust it into his hand. "Look! It's another library! We're going to find more of these all along this wall, I just know it! It was around here we found the scroll ends and scraps of vellum. They must have come from destroyed niches—the ones at this level were protected by the way the roof first fell, then the walls came down on top of it all!"

John saw a small gap in the rubble, just wide enough for the narrow beam of light to show him something of what lay beyond. He could easily make out a compartment about eighteen inches deep and approximately ten inches wide. Fine debris half filled the space between the slabs of smooth-cut stone, partially hiding the long shapes of scroll cases, the wood and leather preserved in the dry atmosphere sealed inside the niche.

John's excitement owed nothing to his MI6 mission. "You know, I think you might be right." He handed Anahita back her torch and rose to his feet, studying the excavated area. "I don't envy you the job of getting them out and stabilizing them, but when you do..."

"You'll be first in line to translate them." She laughed.

"I wish. They're your babies, Anahita. They'll go back to Dushanbe and your department."

"I think we both know you're a lot more

proficient in early medieval Persian than I am," she said quietly. "Or than anyone back at the University or the Museum. I'm going to suggest they hire you to work on them," she added. "When the dig is finished, of course. I'm confident they'll listen to me."

"Thank you," he said sincerely. He wouldn't be able to take the position should it be offered, but the thought gave him a warm feeling.

John was so engrossed in the painstaking work of excavating the fallen tiles without disturbing the contents of the niches behind them, he nearly fell over when a strange voice said, "Hi." He regained his equilibrium and glanced up over his shoulder.

"Hello," Anahita responded, but John barely heard her.

"Ma'am," the man said, smiling and tipping a nonexistent hat. He was crouched on the planks protecting the edge of the trench. Aviator shades hid his eyes, but his smile was wide and bright. Sun-streaked blond hair curled over his forehead and onto the collar of his blue T-shirt, both emphasizing his tan. He was in his early to mid-twenties, ridiculously good-looking, and not one of the students. A camera hung around his neck. Babcock's tame photographer, then. And, irritatingly, he was on his own, no Babcock in sight, and no escort either. John scowled, unwilling to admit to the immediate attraction pulling at him, or the pleasant warmth of incipient arousal in his groin. It was an added complication he didn't need and he couldn't allow his libido to get in his way. His solution was simple; a prickly defense kept away all kinds of trouble.

"So where's Babcock?" John demanded. "I thought he was supposed to show up again."

"Uh, yeah, but something came up and

he sent me instead. I gotta report back to him."

"You shouldn't be on site without an escort," he said curtly.

The man's smile didn't waver. "Yeah, I know I need a watchdog." It was a pleasant drawl, redolent of the American Southwest, and it did nothing to cool John's blood. "I'm trying to find one. Scott Landon." He held out his hand.

John planted his hands on his hips and ignored the offered courtesy. "Go over to the building and wait for Professor Preston. He'll allocate someone to assist you."

"Been there, done that," Scott said cheerfully. "No one showed."

"I expect he's busy," Anahita piped up. "I'll go and see if I can find him for you."

"Thank you, ma'am." But he made no move to return to the offices and wait for Mike.

Scott didn't know what impulse drew

him to the trench inside the ruins, but he was
grateful for it when the man straightened and
turned to face him. He was tall, lean, and sun-
browned, his almost-black hair worn a little too
long and showing a few threads of silver at the
temples, though he was probably under forty.
Deeply set in high-cheekboned, hawk-like
features, dark brown eyes gazed stonily at Scott.
Somehow the man managed to give the
impression of glaring down his impressive,
aquiline nose despite his head being on a level
with Scott's knees. While not strictly handsome,
his was the most interesting face Scott had seen
in years, and also the most attractive. Right
now, however, that face was the personification
of aloofness. A warm pulse of interest spread
through Scott's blood. Never one to pass up a
challenge, he waited until the woman took
herself off then gave the man a thorough
checking out from behind the mask of his

shades.

"So," Scott said brightly, "what do you have here?"

"A trench," he bit out, his rich voice becoming more clipped. "Wait by the offices, Mr Landon."

"Okay," he said, not moving. "But please call me Scott. Mr Landon's my father and it's way too formal for me." He widened his smile to an out and out grin, as charming and engaging as he could make it. "Hey, c'mon, you need to loosen up. I'm not like Brent, I swear. Can I come down there?"

"I do not need to do anything, Mr Landon," the man said icily, "and no, you can't. Go away."

Scott sighed, and wondered what the man's mouth would be like when it wasn't pressed into a thin line. Of course, he might not be gay, but he wouldn't be the first so-called straight guy whom Scott persuaded sexual experimentation was a good idea, though he might be the most difficult. Nor was the setting ideal for seduction. But, as Scott reminded himself, a faint heart never won tall, dark, and interesting.

The woman hurried back toward them, an even taller, harassed-looking man on her heels. Scott stood up to meet them. This had to be the boss man. He gave Scott a friendly smile.

"Mike Preston, Site Director," he introduced himself, and they shook hands.

"Scott Landon."

"Good to meet you, Mr Landon. Mr Babcock's not with you?" The SD was as English as the man in the trench, but, to Scott's relief, a lot more approachable.

"The name's Scott, and thanks. He couldn't make it, but I appreciate the chance to take a look at what you've got going on here. I'll do my best not to get in anyone's way."

"Good, good. Well, until I get clearance, I can't allow you to take photos. Not yet. It's only a formality, but I'm sure you know how it is."

"Sure, no problem." Scott smiled. "I'll behave, I promise." He held up his hand. "Scout's honor." Did he hear a snort from the vicinity of the trench?

"Okay, then. Let's see… John, would you mind giving Scott an overview?"

"Yes, I would. Mike, there are important finds coming up here. Anahita and I want to get the area properly cleared so we can do the recording before we start to move them."

"It's all right, John," the woman said quickly. "I'm sure it won't take you long to give Mr Landon a quick tour." Scott beamed gratefully at her and she blinked, her own smile widening.

"Damn it, Mike!"

"Good, good," Mike said again, briskly rubbing his hands together. "That's settled then. Scott, Doctor Jones is my Assistant Site Director. You'll be in very good, very knowledgeable hands."

"I don't doubt it," Scott replied demurely, gazing down through his lashes at the irritated face below him. This time the snort of disgust sounded loud and clear as the man turned on his heel and strode for the ladder. He climbed up quickly and with an intriguingly smooth economy of movement. "Hi, again," Scott said when they were face to face, but he didn't make the mistake of offering to shake hands a second time. They were the same height, though the archaeologist had a lighter build. "Can I call you John?"

"No. Come on, let's get this over with."

Scott shrugged, unabashed. Anahita

offered him an embarrassed smile and he winked at her. "Hey," he whispered in passing, "after a couple of months with Babcock, your Doc's all sweetness and light." She was surprised into a giggle, and he trotted after the fast-walking archaeologist, taking the opportunity to check out the man's taut ass as he did so.

Doctor Jones led him away from the site, up the dusty track to the apology of a road, then stopped and turned to gesture back down to the site. And started talking.

This was literally the overview. Scott expected minimal information, a sketchy description of the site and its history. Instead he received a full-blown lecture on medieval trade routes, politics, sponsors, and banking that left him in something of an information-overloaded daze. John Jones obviously intended to bore the bejesus out of him, but he failed. The man possessed a natural talent with words and his love of his subjects came through in every phrase. A lot of the historical minutiae sailed over Scott's head, but the deep, expressive voice held him spellbound, and enough facts lodged in his overheated brain to let him ask some reasonably intelligent questions. At the same time, he was framing shots in his head, noting the way the caravanserai fit into the landscape, how the westering sun and the lengthening shadows painted the ruined walls and the irregular checkerboard of trenches, how the colorful tent village on its plateau looked almost medieval in its own right. But one more question burned on his tongue.

"I don't get it," Scott blurted. "I mean, I know why Brent's doing the Silk Roads. We've spent the last couple of months traveling some of the shittiest roads I've seen, staying in places I wouldn't stable a goat, and eating crappy food.

At the end of it he'll have a book guaranteed to hit the best sellers' list and make him a load of cash. I went to Peru with Felipe Hermanes— he's a journalist and into conservation—because he wanted to explore and record what he could of the rainforest before the loggers obliterated it, and use his book to raise enough awareness so there'd be more of an effort to stop the destruction of the rainforest. So, okay, I understand the difference between commercialism and protecting the planet. But you, these kids, you're out here in a strange land, living in tents with basic amenities, no real freedom to come and go, watched over every now and then by the army. Just to dig holes in the ground. *Why?* What's the point of it?"

"*Why?*" John rounded on him ferociously, taking Scott's breath away. "Do you think we live in a vacuum? That present and future are the be-all and end-all of two-dimensional lives? The point is, Mr Landon, you, me, those postgraduates, the lecturers, the cooks and drivers, are linked to the past as surely as we are to the present. We are no different from the people who traveled the Roads and stayed in the caravanserai. We are no different from the Roman soldier on Hadrian's Wall who wrote home to his mother asking her to send him more socks. And yes, before you ask, he's genuine. Every minute fragment of the past found in excavations enriches the present. Every translation of newly discovered writing expands our knowledge and strengthens the links to our past. Human nature has changed very little in the millennia we've walked upright, and we're faced with the same choices today as our ancestors were. The only differences now are our enhanced abilities to create and destroy."

The words seemed to sear themselves into his brain and take root. Scott gazed at John, mouth parted, eyes wide, completely ensnared by the man's passion and not a little turned on by it. "Wow," he breathed. John's color rose and he turned away, his mouth in a thin, uncompromising line. "You give one hell of a speech."

The archaeologist didn't answer, just strode on down the track, leaving Scott to trot after him.

"Can I see some of the finds?" he asked as they returned to the excavations, more interested in prolonging the time he spent with the man than a desire to see the excavated stuff.

"I suppose so," John agreed reluctantly, and detoured to the building.

The main room was large, lined with long tables covered with labeled trays and charts of the trenches. Another bank of tables holding artifacts stretched down its center. It was obviously time for a coffee break safely away from the finds; a handful of young men and women around Scott's age were leaving as they entered, and they all gave John cheerful greetings as they passed. No matter how abrasive the man was toward stray photographers, he seemed popular with the students. For Scott, it proved the man possessed another, more approachable side. Now he had to find it and close in.

"So the quake hit," he said, "and then what? They just pulled out?"

"Yes. As far as we can tell, the people stayed for a short time, salvaging what they could, rescuing the living, burying the dead. We've found no bodies so far, apart from the skeletons of a couple of mules under the rubble. We haven't found the cemetery yet, either. But we haven't been authorized to excavate it in any case. Just the caravanserai itself."

Scott looked around at the trays and their contents. Most contained pottery, unidentifiable pieces of rusted iron, verdigrised bronze and copper, some brightly glazed tiles, coins, small carved objects, and bits of bright metal filigree. "Is this gold?" he asked, touching one small, crumpled piece.

"Yes. It's part of a scroll case. It would have been attached to ivory slats. There's a more intact one over here." Scott joined him by another tray. Narrow strips of ivory lay side by side, slender lengths of delicate gold filigree-work still in place on some of them. Others were delicately carved with similar designs. The artistry took his breath away.

"Wow," Scott said with a wonder he didn't have to fake. "A high status thing, then?"

"Very. It was found in the mosque, and would probably have contained a religious text. Scroll cases were more usually made of pottery, wood, or leather." John glanced pointedly at his watch, and Scott guessed the lecture tour was over. It was time to make his move.

"Thanks for this," he said sincerely. "It's been fascinating. Really. Do you get the chance to go into Ishkoshim?"

The archaeologist seemed slightly taken aback by the abrupt change of conversation. "Occasionally. Why?"

Scott took a couple of steps forward, bringing him right into John's personal space. The man's eyes were peat-brown, dark and deep, and he smelled faintly of *Element*, the cologne Scott favored for himself. It was slightly different on John. Warmer, but still recognizable. "How about we meet up there?" he suggested, his smile inviting. "Have coffee, talk, just the two of us?"

Startlement became shock became outrage. "Landon, are you propositioning me?"

he hissed.

"What? Propo—whoever says that these days? I'm coming on to you. How about it, Doc?"

"Absolutely not!"

"Why not?" Scott refused to give ground, and John didn't seem prepared to push past him.

"Because," the man snarled, "you are the same age as those kids out there—young enough to be my son—and I don't fuck children. Am I being clear enough for you, Landon? Now get out of my way before my fist comes on to your jaw!"

"Bullshit!" Scott snorted, but he decided discretion was the better part of valor and backed away. "You're years younger than my dad. I don't buy it."

"Get out!"

"I am. Out and proud. I wear rainbow

boxer-briefs—"

Hands clenched into fists, John took one long, lithe stride toward him. Scott dodged around a table, putting it between himself and the angry man, suddenly aware the archaeologist could actually be dangerous. "But I'm not into BDSM," he continued, edging for the door, "especially the SM, so I'll leave you to it. If you change your mind about the coffee, just let me know." He bolted out the door like a jackrabbit, a shit-eating grin spreading wide.

John hadn't proclaimed himself straight.

## CHAPTER THREE

The door slammed shut on Scott's fast exit, and John slowly relaxed. *Damn the man!* But at least Scott would have gotten the message loud and clear: he was not interested. Period. But for a traitorous moment, John's blood heated and rushed south. If he'd been no one but his surface persona, and there hadn't been Gulab and the tribal treaties to be handled with kid gloves, then perhaps he would have taken the idiot up on his offer regardless of the age difference. There was something about the man... He'd discovered over the last hour that Scott possessed a lively intelligence and imagination, and a vibrant energy added to his appeal. He hadn't been driven away by the avalanche of detail thrown at him; on the contrary, he even seemed to have absorbed some of it.

The growl of an engine reached him, and he assumed it was Scott being driven back to the town. John resolutely put the photographer out of his mind. He couldn't afford the distraction. Right then the absent Brent Babcock and his awkward questions were foremost in his thoughts. He decided he needed a large mug of coffee, so he headed for the mess tent.

All too soon John discovered he'd made the wrong choice. Scott sat with Anahita and a small group of students, mostly female. The photographer seemed to be recounting an anecdote, and by the frequent bursts of giggles, it was a comical one.

"—So Brent backs off, zipping up," Scott said, glancing up and meeting John's gaze, "and Azad's granddaddy says, 'Yeah, you better be careful, my goats will eat anything'."

Hoots of laughter rang out, and Scott's smile seemed to be welcoming as well as amused. Anahita moved over to make space on the bench she shared with him, but John declined it with a smile of his own and a shake of his head. Instead, he made a beeline for the industrial-sized coffeemaker. Irritatingly, Scott joined him to refill his own mug.

"These kids are great," Scott said brightly. "And they like you. Come and join us."

"These kids are the same age as you," John snapped.

"You don't know that. It could be I just look younger than I am. Plastic surgery," he added, nodding wisely. "Botox."

"Idiot," John muttered, keeping his expression blank though he badly wanted to laugh.

"Okay, so I'm twenty-five. Well, almost. Still too old to be your son. A nephew, maybe. If you have an older brother. Or sister. And I'm not a greenhorn fresh out of college. I've been doing gigs with journalists for the last four years. Learned my trade that way, not in lecture halls and art galleries."

"Really. I am overwhelmed with disinterest."

"Y'know, for a guy who obviously has above-average intelligence, you're kinda dumb."

*"What?"*

"Ain't it dawned on you the more yah play hard to get, the more Ah'm gonna chase?" Scott said in a lazy drawl straight out of a John Wayne western. "See yah, Doc." Then he strolled away with a swagger to his shoulders, but not before he gave John's backside a surreptitious and exploratory pat. Luckily Scott's body hid the brief contact, and John managed not to react to it, though he would have liked to throw the man out of the mess tent.

"Idiot," he repeated under his breath, and

took his coffee back to his own tent for a brief respite. A few more hours of daylight remained before work ended for the day, and if they were lucky, he and Anahita would get the recording done. Then what might be only the first cache of scrolls could be carefully moved to the conservation room. But more importantly, he needed to know what Babcock was up to.

John gave himself ten minutes to write up some notes on the tablets already recovered from the site and to drink his coffee before he returned to Anahita's trench. She joined him on the way with a friendly smile. A single sweeping glance revealed Scott being shepherded to the far side of the dig by the quartet of female students. By the look of it, he was getting another tour, this time unofficial.

"He's nice," Anahita said as she paused and followed his gaze. "The photographer. I don't think he'll be inappropriate with the girls. He's so much nicer than that reporter." John grunted but made no other comment. She didn't need any encouragement. "Such pretty hair, and a lovely smile..."

"I'll take your word for it," he answered lightly. "I think we're going to need a few extra pairs of hands here if we're to get everything done and those scrolls out before we finish for the day. I'll go and have a word with Mike, see who we can borrow."

"Good idea," she replied. He left her at the trench and picked his way across toward the sieving center by the spoil heap and Mike's tall figure.

His path took him past the battered truck he'd been traveling in earlier. The hood was up and Azad was tinkering with the engine, swearing in his native Tajik. John didn't pause or glance at the man, just took out his handkerchief and mopped his face. "Any update on Babcock?" he asked, the fabric hiding his mouth.

"Yes, and you won't like it," Azad replied amid a stream of insults snarled at the truck. "He's talking to some of Mazdak's sympathizers, but Daryush can't find out what answers he's getting. Yet. We'll stay on it."

John passed the handkerchief over his brow one more time and continued walking.

\* \* \* \*

"Where the hell have you been?" Babcock snapped. Scott shut the door behind him and strolled into Babcock's shabby room in Ishkoshim's only guesthouse. His own room, smaller and even more Spartan, was across the narrow hall.

"Checking out the dig, like you said," he

answered.

"Did it have to take you all this fucking time?"

"Yes. It pays to be sociable, Brent. They're an interesting bunch." He helped himself to an unopened bottle of water sitting on the rickety table under the window and looked out over the street. The usual Border Guard patrols were out there, young men—teenagers most of them—carrying AK47s. Another Ishkoshim sat on the Afghanistan side of the Panj River, a smaller, more rundown version of its Tajik twin.

"Get any shots?"

"Not yet. Mike Preston said he'll let me know when he gets clearance from Dushanbe."

Babcock glared at him. "You could have sneaked some. Forget it. I want the dramatic shots—the students working under the guns of the Tajik military. You hang around until you get them."

"Okay," Scott said placidly. He saw no point in wasting his breath so he didn't bother to remark that such a photo would give an entirely false image of the situation. Besides, it gave him a great excuse to work on his own personal project: John Jones. "Did you have any luck?"

"Did I ever." Babcock gave a short bark of laughter. "The Taliban are moving in on some of the tribal leaders—Shaheen Jalil for one, and he's pressuring Mazdak Rudaki. This whole region could go to hell in a hand basket." He grinned, fiercely satisfied. "That's one hell of a story, Scotty."

A queasy kind of certainty grew in Scott's gut, swamping the irritation triggered by the nickname. "So what are you planning?" he asked eagerly. He was no stranger to dangerous assignments, even if those hadn't involved guns, and so far this Silk Road exploration had turned out to be comparatively tame.

"Nothing's settled yet. You concentrate on the dig and getting in with Preston and Jones. But be ready to come running when I give the signal. We may have to put the Silk Road on hold, but it'll be worth it. This is gonna be huge. And risky. Are you up for it?"

"Sure," Scott said easily, the sudden surge of adrenaline kicking in to settle his stomach.

"Good man."

"So what's the plan?"

"Uh-uh." Babcock shook his head. "What you don't know you can't tell."

"Shit, Brent!" But the man would not say more, and Scott went to his bed frustrated in more ways than one.

The journalist and their rented car were gone early the next morning, before Scott woke up. So he had a few words with Housyar, the glum-featured man who cooked, served meals, and booked travelers in and out. Half an hour later, Scott rode away on an ancient Honda motorcycle.

Despite its wheezing, coughs, and backfires, the bike got him to the excavation site in time to join the tail end of the breakfast queue, to his relief. The food at the guesthouse was edible, but didn't come up to the standard supplied to the students.

The two Site Directors and a familiar lecturer—Anahita, he'd learned yesterday—occupied a table in a corner, and an unclaimed chair sat between her and Mike. Scott wandered over and hovered hopefully.

"Mind if I join you?" he asked Mike, ignoring John and his frown for the time being.

"Not at all," came the cheerful reply. "You're an unexpectedly bright and early arrival. It's far too soon for me to have heard anything from Dushanbe about your photography."

"No problem." Scott offered his best disingenuous smile. "I do have an ulterior motive, though," he added, and managed not to glance at the Assistant Site Director.

"I'll bet," John muttered under Mike's amused, "Oh?"

"Yeah. Uh, well, first John here, and then some of the postgrads, showed me around and talked about the site, the things you're finding, excavation techniques, and—" He broke off with a self-depreciating shrug. "Well, it kinda hooked me. Brent's taken off on a story lead of his own, so I'm at loose ends. Is there any chance I could—I don't know—help out around here?"

"Not a good idea," John said predictably enough.

"Scott, I wish I could say yes," said Mike, genuinely regretful.

"Oh, not down in the trenches excavating stuff. But there must be some grunt work I could do. Carry buckets, push wheelbarrows, bring water bottles to the diggers?"

"Perhaps. I'll think about it," Mike replied, and John said nothing more. His frown spoke for him.

"But you must not distract the students," Anahita said severely, though her dark eyes twinkled.

She meant don't flirt with the girls, and Scott put his hand on his heart. "Word of honor," he said with perfect sincerity. "I won't." No, he had quite a different goal in mind.

"So when can we expect Babcock to arrive and brighten our lives?" John asked with a mildness that did nothing to hide his exasperation.

"Sorry, I've got no idea. He's on the track of something hot, and he's keeping it to himself."

"Hm," Mike said, a worried frown on his usually good-natured features. "Might be a little dodgy for him. Asking about the Silk Roads and the dig is one thing, involving himself in local situations could turn nasty really quickly. The soldiers can be a little trigger-happy."

"Not to mention the civilians," John added dryly.

"Situations?" Scott asked innocently. It was one of his best expressions.

"Drug smuggling," Anahita whispered, resting her hand on his. "Gunrunning, smuggling rubies, other gems. This is a border village, remember, and the people are poor. Over the river, they're even more so. There are always some who will do almost anything for money and power. And religious belief. Please tell him to be careful and keep away from all of it."

"Anahita's right," John said. "Hotheads probably won't bother to discriminate between helpless students and intrusive journalists." He sounded serious, with not a trace of sarcasm. "If he wants to risk his life—and yours—that's the choice you both make. But these postgraduates are our concern."

Scott nodded. "I hear you," he said soberly. And he did, for the first time stopping to think what repercussions there might be against Westerners in general. "I'll have a word with him when I see him next." But he didn't hold out much hope he could make Babcock change his mind.

Scott didn't dwell on the problem overmuch. He hadn't been entirely lying about his fascination with the site and archaeology, and when Mike finally gave him the go-ahead, Scott was only too pleased to make himself useful. The Site Director assigned him to the four-man squad working in a wide trench taking in the footings of the small mosque and the courtyard in front of it. They were glad of the extra set of muscles for the tedious but necessary wheelbarrow and bucket duty, and were happy to talk about the finds turning up in their trench. It didn't hurt that John worked in the next trench over.

It didn't take much for Scott to occasionally nudge the postgrads' casual chatting onto the subject of their lecturers, and by the afternoon he'd learned a little more about Doctor John Jones—that he was unmarried, unpartnered, well-liked and respected, and very much a newcomer. Which surprised Scott; the man came across as a seamlessly integral part of the senior-level team, and he'd assumed John had been there right from the start. On his way to the spoil heap with another couple of buckets, Scott glanced over at the trench by the inner wall.

No one showed above the rim; the working surface was at least four feet down, but he could hear people talking and the steady scraping of trowels. Two of the voices were high-pitched, excited babbles of Russian. Anahita and one of her students had found more scrolls, Scott guessed, smiling. Then came John's voice, rich and warmly resonant, tugging at him on all kinds of different levels. But Scott summoned up his willpower and trudged on toward the steadily expanding pile of excavated soil. It would be a very bad idea to put the moves on the man in public, given their location. Most of the students probably wouldn't give a damn, but there were others who might. The locals hired to support the dig would almost certainly carry the story of man-on-man action back to their homes and villages, and sooner or later someone would object with traditional violence. Flogging and/or stoning did not make appearances in Scott's fantasies, erotic or otherwise.

As he started back to the mosque trench, a general movement began all over the site. People were standing, stretching backs and arms and legs. In twos and threes, the students headed for the mess tent. Mid-afternoon break, then. His team of postgrads passed him on their way and one of them, Jacques, invited him along. Scott noticed Anahita and her companion were moving as well. John, on the other hand, wasn't.

When a swift glance around showed Scott everyone else had disappeared into the mess tent, he strolled over to the trench.

John had just started to climb the ladder. Sweat sheened his skin, dampening his hair to black curls on his forehead, and as far as Scott was concerned the man looked good enough to eat. He probably wouldn't get another chance at this, so he dropped to his knees on the plank at the edge of the trench. As John raised his head to stare at him in surprise, Scott leaned down and covered his mouth in a deep, tongue-probing kiss. John started to jerk away, nearly fell off the rungs, then snatched one-handed at Scott's shirt. But not to retain his balance. Instead he twisted his grip into the fabric and held Scott in place, taking over the kiss with fierce concentration. Scott's joints melted and lava-heat spread through his veins. John's tongue licked possessively deep, dancing over Scott's teeth and the roof of his mouth, and a whimper of pure need escaped Scott's throat. Fire sparked along his nerves, surged through his body on a tide of pure lust. Then he was thrust away so forcefully he ended up sprawled on his side in the dust.

"Idiot!" the archaeologist snarled. He climbed up the ladder and strode off toward the mess tent.

Scott fell back, head thunking on the hard ground, a silly grin on his face, and a happy swelling in his pants. His lips were swollen, blood zipped through his body, and every nerve was tingling. "God," he said to the sky. "I have got to do that again."

He didn't attempt to catch up with John, sensible enough to realize he'd most likely get a verbal lashing that would lift metaphoric strips off him, if not a fist in the face. Instead, he was content to amble along in the man's wake, enjoying the hinted-at bunch and glide of muscle under the dusty fabric of John's slacks.

## CHAPTER FOUR

For what remained of his day on the dig, Scott kept out of John's way, not wishing to push his luck. Even without his success in stealing the kiss, he'd had a good time. The work was hard, but he was on the edge of the ongoing developments and found them fascinating. The icing on his cake came from Mike, just as Scott was making his farewells.

"I've just got an email from Dushanbe," the Site Director said. "You're cleared for photography, but you check each shot with me or John, we review the ones you've taken, and you only keep the ones we approve."

"Sounds good to me," Scott smiled. "Thanks, Mike. It's okay if I come back tomorrow and work as well as photograph?"

"Of course. We'll be glad to see you, and thanks for your help today."

Scott waved a casual salute and bullied the motorcycle into life, heading back to Ishkoshim. It had been a good day. A very good day. His lips could still feel the pressure of John's kiss and the probing tongue seemingly intent on mapping every interior millimeter of Scott's mouth. If it wasn't for the sometimes painful jolts as the bike bounced from pothole to pothole, Scott would have spent the ride with a semi-permanent erection.

Babcock was lying in wait for him. As Scott passed the coffee shop next door to the guesthouse, the journalist barreled out and waved him down.

"We're on," Babcock said before Scott could say a word. Suppressed excitement harshened the man's voice to a hoarse whisper, for which Scott was thankful. This conversation shouldn't be overheard. "I got a meeting set up with Mazdak Rudaki. He's a tribal leader based to the north of here, and he's pivotal to what goes on in the whole region."

"Uh, Brent," Scott said, uneasily remembering the conversation in the mess tent. "Are you sure this is a good idea?"

"Getting cold feet, Scotty?" he sneered. "This is a major break, for fuck's sake!"

"I know!" Scott snapped, stung by the insult as well as the nickname. "You do realize there are a lot of Western targets out on the dig if this backfires on us."

"It isn't going to backfire. No one's going to bother with the archaeologists; they bring too much trade and kudos to the village."

"Tell that to the families of some of the aid workers in Afghanistan," Scott countered. "What else do we know about this Mazdak guy?"

"I told you. From what I've found out,

he's one of the foremost chiefs around here. He says jump, they ask how high. Someone will come for us at midnight, and we'll be back before dawn, with no one the wiser. Okay?"

"Okay," Scott answered, eagerness and adrenaline rush combining uncomfortably with images of the defenseless postgraduates—and John's concerned expression.

"Knew I could count on you, Scotty. Midnight. Go get some rest."

At midnight they sneaked out the back door of the guesthouse to find a tall shadow waiting for them. The man greeted them in Russian, which Scott did not speak and wished he did, and they were ushered to the back of an old, ex-Soviet army truck. The engine was idling quietly, the sound surprisingly healthy given the state of the vehicle's metalwork. As soon as they were aboard, the canvas door was drawn closed and the truck pulled away. They weren't in complete darkness; Scott could see the dim shapes of four men as he climbed in, all of them smoking rank cigarettes. Chain-smoking, he realized, as the regular flare of matches showed him impassive, bearded faces. Babcock chatted to them in fluent Russian, and they answered him readily enough. They seemed relaxed, certainly weren't hostile. If anything, his brief glimpses of them showed they were faintly amused by whatever Babcock was spouting at them, and Scott let himself unwind a little. Until he thought about it and realized their companions were too relaxed, too smugly confident.

"Hey, Brent," he started quietly then second-guessed himself. The Tajiks might speak English. He took a chance the journalist knew Spanish and said in a cheerful voice, "*Tengo un mal presentimiento...*" *I have a bad feeling...*

"What?" Scott got the impression Babcock turned toward him. "*Qué quieres decir?*" *What do you mean?*

"Our pals are too sure of themselves," he answered in Spanish. "This just doesn't feel right to me."

There was a long stretch of silence. Then, "Don't be dumb." But the man didn't sound so confident. One of the Tajiks struck another match and held it, his features a scowling, demonic mask in the fitful light. He barked something at Babcock, who laughed and answered briefly.

"*Qué?*" Scott asked nervously.

"I told 'em what I keep telling you. You're a dumb jerk who can't remember English half the time." He switched to Spanish. "Maybe you're right, maybe not. But be ready to make a break for it if we have to. I'm carrying."

Scott chuckled and hoped it didn't sound

as false to the Tajiks as it did to him. He was unarmed but for his Swiss Army knife. Somehow he didn't believe the God-knows-how-many gadgets on it were going to be much help.

The ride became increasingly rough. The truck scrambled, jounced, bucked, and rocked its way across appallingly bad terrain, and Scott was sure they couldn't be following a trail of any kind. He hung onto the grab-rails for dear life and wondered how the hell they were going to get out of this if his gut instinct proved correct. Then after one more spine-wrenching jolt, they were traveling on a comparatively level surface. A short while later the truck braked to a juddering halt.

Almost before the vehicle stopped moving, two of the Tajiks shoved aside the tarp and jumped down. Flickering firelight illuminated the interior of the truck, gleaming on the AK47s as the remaining pair stood up. But the guns were slung over the men's shoulders, no obvious immediate threat to anyone. Babcock snorted in disgust and glared at Scott.

"Jumping at shadows, greenhorn?" he muttered.

"Out," one of the men ordered, and Babcock got to his feet, using Scott's shoulder for leverage.

"Mazdak better be worth it," the journalist growled. "This heap of fucking junk has just about busted every bone I got."

"Brent!" Scott whispered desperately. "This is gonna—"

"Can it!" Babcock elbowed past him and clambered out of the truck—to be grabbed by the arms and forced to the ground, his wrists pulled up toward his shoulder blades before he could do more than yelp in shock and pain. At the same time, Scott sensed sudden movement behind him. He spun around, fist swinging. The butt of a gun cracked against the side of his head and he staggered, his punch going wide. Dazed though he was, Scott lurched forward and wrapped his arms around the man's thighs in a clumsy football tackle. His attack took the man by surprise, Scott's weight and momentum enough to bring them both down in the cramped confines of the truck. The second gunman yelled what had to be curses, stabbing his gun butt at Scott's head and ribs, while Scott wrestled for his opponent's weapon. Another Tajik joined in, climbing into the truck and throwing himself onto Scott's back. The force of the newcomer's landing knocked the breath from Scott's lungs. When a forearm locked around his throat, Scott knew he'd lost the battle. But he didn't stop struggling until blackness swamped him.

\* \* \* \*

It wasn't often anyone managed to surprise John, but Scott Landon had pulled it off. John rolled over on his pallet mattress and resettled the sleeping bag over his shoulders. He'd unzipped the thing to use it as a quilt, and tonight every toss and turn started it sliding to the floor. The replays of Scott's kiss made sure there were plenty of both. Up to then he'd been certain Scott was just indulging in a harmless but irritating flirtation—well, harmless as long as it was kept out of the sight of the more intolerant, and irritating because John was on an assignment and couldn't take Scott up on his blatant offer even if the man wasn't fourteen years younger. But for Scott to actually land a kiss on him was completely out of order.

Anger and arousal hummed through John's blood. He should have punched the bastard. Frozen him off. Done anything other than kiss him back. Unbidden, the memory replayed: the pressure of Scott's lips, the wet heat of his tongue... his mouth when John invaded it and the hungry sound he'd made before John thrust him away. Then there was the lively intelligence behind those blue eyes, the cocky humor, the sheer vitality of the man... For an instant John experienced an almost overwhelming need to know more about Scott, to explore his vibrant personality as well as his powerful, young body.

Young. Twenty-four to John's thirty-eight. Even if he didn't work for MI6, the age gap— John cut off the thought and turned over. Okay, Scott wasn't quite young enough to be his son, but the years separating them precluded—

He rolled onto his back, snatching at the sleeping bag too late to prevent it ending up on the floor of the tent. John swore under his breath and yanked the bag over him again. Since joining MI6, he'd been very wary of entering into a relationship of any kind. He'd seen the destructive tension the absolute need for secrecy could cause between friends, let alone lovers. Then there was the ever-present possibility that threats to someone close could be used as leverage, to coerce him to hand over information.

John knew he was making a mountain out of a molehill. The randy young stud spent too much time away from civilization with the likes of Brent Babcock, so the only thing on his agenda was a fast fuck to scratch the itch. John had no intention of indulging him. But the way he'd responded to Scott's kiss couldn't be called discouragement by any stretch of the imagination.

His arousal refused to go away. John turned over once more. He would not pander to his body's demands, now or later. Tomorrow he'd make sure Scott got the message that he, John Jones, was off-limits and unavailable.

\* \* \* \*

"I think Scott isn't quite as keen as he seemed yesterday," Mike said, mild disappointment in his voice.

"Mm?" John looked up from the latest tablets sitting in the finds tray beside Anahita's trench. "Y'know, it might not be another library. These aren't religious tracts, they're letters, bills of lading." Then he registered Mike's words. "Scott? What about him?"

"He hasn't shown up."

"You're surprised?"

"Cynic. Yves says Jacques and his team found him really useful, and from what I could see, he didn't back off from hard work."

"I'm sure," John said dryly. He glanced at his watch: nearly midday. "Still, we should be thankful for small blessings—Babcock isn't here, either." Then he frowned, suddenly wondering why both men were absent. If the journalist had taken off in search of his other story despite their warnings, and taken Scott with him, there wasn't anything he could do about it.

"Damn it, you don't think—?" Mike began worriedly, clearly on the same wavelength.

John shrugged. "Maybe. Babcock seemed bullheaded enough to ignore sensible advice, but I suspect he's well able to take care of himself."

"But Scott's just a kid."

"Hardly," John answered. "He's the same age as the postgrads, but he hasn't spent his life in a comparatively sheltered university environment. He's been out in the real world."

"I suppose," Mike said reluctantly.

"You," John said with a smile, "are a mother hen. He'll show up, I'm sure, bold as brass and twice as cocky."

Mike muttered something under his breath, and John returned to the tablets, his smile fading as Mike walked away. Uneasiness settled under his ribs; concern, he told himself, in case the idiot—both idiots—walked into a situation that might rebound on the archaeologists. A searching glance around the site told him Daryush and Azad weren't there either. For both men to be absent at the same time was unusual, and he hadn't forgotten Gulab Turi's warning.

The day wore on. More clay tablets came out of Anahita's trench, and Mike detailed a small team of students to assist her, freeing up

John to put in more work on the translations. John also made several patrols of the site, ostensibly examining finds but in reality on the lookout for his two contacts. They remained absent and John spent the rest of his time in his office, copying and translating the steadily growing number of tablets and stabilized scrolls. Fascinating though the work was, it did not distract him. The photographer sat at the forefront of his thoughts, along with the journalist and John's mission.

He had a very strong hunch the wheel was about to fall off his wagon.

Late in the afternoon, a squad of Border Guards appeared on the heights above the site, the first time they'd put in an appearance since John's arrival. None of the archaeologists paid the uniformed figures much attention, and the soldiers didn't come any closer to the dig. By the time everyone filed into the mess tent for the evening meal, they were gone. John breathed a sigh of relief. The military presence was probably a coincidence, but his hunch only set its teeth a little deeper into his nerves.

John had been an agent for too long to ignore his instincts, but he didn't break his usual routine. After dinner he walked the site with Mike and the other lecturers, discussing the day's finds, and then put in another hour or two in the office. When night fell and the generators chugged quietly in the background, powering the lights in the building and the tent village, someone lit the fire in the large brazier standing in the open space in front of the mess tent. Soon figures gathered 'round the flames for the evening socializing. Music started up, covering the sounds of the generators but not loud enough to be intrusive. All was as it should be.

John unzipped his tent's door, went

inside, and rezipped it behind him. Site etiquette meant the closed door would be respected. No one would pay him a visit while it remained shut. Enough light seeped through the tent walls for him to see without being silhouetted. He removed his satphone from its hiding place in the lining of his suitcase, but before he could turn it on and key in the number, a faint scratching caught his attention. It came from the sleeping compartment. Or seemed to. When he cautiously unfastened the door and peered in, he saw no one.

The scratching came again, from outside at the back of the tent, and a quiet voice, no more than a whisper, said, "There is a problem."

John sat on the edge of his bed and leaned forward. "Azad," he murmured. "Tell me it's not the Americans."

"It's them. They left the guesthouse in the night. I didn't see them go. Word is they were going to a meeting arranged with Mazdak but he took them prisoner. He's going to send them to the Taliban as a token of his support. What do you want us to do?"

"Damn it!" John didn't ask how Azad discovered it. The brothers had their own network among the locals. "Do you know where they are?"

"Yes, I'm sure of their location. Unless they've been moved since I tracked them."

John nodded. "Good enough for me. Where's Daryush?"

"Not far away. He's got transport and kit for you, just in case."

"Good. Give me a minute. I'm going to report in."


Despite the five hour time difference, Maria was alert and on the ball. Moments after explaining the situation to her, John was talking to his Area Director. Boudrier didn't waste time either.

"Get them out," his boss said over the satellite link, the irritation in his voice clear, "before they end up as ransom fodder or cause an international incident. Do what you have to do, but keep Gulab Turi on our side and don't blow your cover." The order came as no surprise, but obeying would be easier said than done.

John ended the call and thought for a moment, juggling scenarios in his head. "Okay," he whispered to Azad. "Take me to Daryush then you get in touch with Gulab. Tell him I'm dealing with the Americans and if he's planning on moving against Mazdak, ask him not to do anything until I get them away."

"As God wills," Azad muttered. "There's only a crescent moon and the ground is rough, so I brought night-vision glasses for us. We should go now."

John took a few moments to change into dark clothing, cursing Babcock under his breath as he did so.

For twenty minutes, John and Azad trekked on foot across southern Tajikistan's more inhospitable countryside, meeting up with Daryush outside a shallow cave. There John put on the clothes Daryush had brought, and checked the wicked-looking knife and handgun provided. Their transport turned out to be four lean ponies, surely more goat than horse.

Azad headed back toward the village while John and Daryush swung into the saddles, gathered up the reins of the two spare mounts, and picked their way over terrain that could have doubled as a moonscape. Any vehicle with wheels would have been defeated at the first rockslide.

## CHAPTER FIVE

With midnight well behind them, they were deep in the next tribal area.

"If we get caught now," Daryush whispered, "we're dog meat."

The monumental understatement won a snort from John. "God, the things I do for MI6," he muttered, scratching at his chest. Daryush had supplied the kind of outfit virtually every Tajik man wore outside of the major towns and cities—a combination of old Soviet Army surplus fatigues and traditional garb. From his skin out, nothing John wore could be traced back to the West, including his handgun, an ex-Russian military issue 9 mm Makarov and the night-vision goggles. The garments, while they were none too clean and probably infested with fleas, proved comfortably warm in the chilly night air.

Daryush sniggered. "You agents are tough. Like James Bond, yes?" It was an old joke between them, one John didn't appreciate right then.

"Oh, yes. No question. Tough as old boots." He tugged his felt and fur cap a little lower and made sure his scarf was tied securely over his nose and mouth. His dark eyes and brows would let him pass as Tajik if anyone got close enough to look past the close-fitting goggles. "How much farther?"

"Over the next ridge. From now on we speak only Tajiki or Russian. The older American speaks Russian."

John nodded, and thanked God one of the captives would be able to follow and translate orders. The chance the journalist would recognize him through his disguise was vanishingly small. Scott might be more of a problem, given his interest in John.

"We'll leave the horses here," Daryush said quietly, breaking into his thoughts. "They're in the deserted settlement, just over the ridge. Azad said they don't have anyone watching this side, just the road up from the valley."

"Not expecting anyone to be daft enough to use horses instead of a truck?"

Daryush grinned. "More fool them."

They slipped between tumbled boulders and semi-desiccated undergrowth, and it was as well they moved as silent as shadows. Azad's information was wrong. As they crested the ridge, the night breeze carried the stench of stale sweat and tobacco to John's nostrils. He froze in his tracks, signaling to Daryush. Ahead of them and off to one side, a dark, boulder-like shape moved slightly and gave a smothered cough. The man wasn't smoking at the moment, but the odor of past cigarettes clung to him. A swift signal from John sent Daryush edging back a short way; he would scout for more sentries while John took out this one.

The man sat on a low rock, his semi-automatic rifle across his lap. He was facing up the slope but he wasn't wearing night glasses. His only light came from the thin sliver of the moon, slowly dropping toward the horizon.

Slowly, aware that time was not on their side, John worked his way around the man's position to come up on him from behind. Sound carried more at night, and John couldn't afford to give away any advantage. He crept close, moving at a snail's pace to minimize the rub of his clothing, breathing through his mouth—and struck at the base of the man's skull. The sentry folded and John snatched the rifle before it could clatter to the ground. With his other arm, he carefully lowered the unconscious sentry to lie sprawled among the rocks.

Daryush joined him and fished a couple

of cable ties from his pockets. "One other man watching," he whispered, handing over the ties. "He's sleeping it off, like this one. I guessed you wouldn't want throats cut."

"You guessed right," John murmured. He cuffed the man's ankles and wrists, linked them together behind his back with the man's own belt then gagged him with his own scarf. "Okay, let's hope they haven't made any more changes since Azad's report."

They sneaked silently down to the huddle of partially ruined huts. According to Azad's information, the prisoners were in the least derelict building. It also stood farthest from the road. The hut's one window faced the hillside and a guard leaned against the wall beside it, the tiny, firefly glow of a lit cigarette hanging from his mouth. He fidgeted, scratched at his crotch, then straightened and propped his rifle beside him. He turned to face the wall, unbuttoning his fly as he did so. The sound and scent of urine hit the air. Daryush took him down with a chokehold in mid-flow and clubbed him unconscious. Moments later, the sentry was trussed up like his colleagues up the hill, and carried off to be hidden among the boulders.

That left one more guard to be dealt with. He sat cross-legged in front of the barred door, swaying slightly, humming tunelessly. As John crept closer he could just about hear the tinny wail coming from the ear buds of the iPod stuck in the bandolier across his chest. Now that was a piece of luck.

The window was an empty square some six feet off the ground, and proved to be just wide enough to let John's shoulders through. He chinned himself up and peered in. Night-vision showed him a green on green image defined by shadows and a flare of brightness; two men tied at the wrists and ankles lay on thin pallets across the single room from each other. The sight of a relatively undamaged Scott sent a surge of relief washing over John, nearly shaking him off balance.

Other than a stinking bucket near the door and a faintly glowing paraffin lantern, there was no furniture. Babcock seemed to be asleep, but Scott wasn't. His focus was solely on the trio of rats paying close attention to some unidentifiable remains on a tin plate.

"Be quiet," John breathed in Russian then repeated it when Scott's head jerked up. He pressed a hand over his own mouth in a universal message and got a short nod in reply. Quickly John hauled himself up and through the window, landing with a slithering thud and rolling to his feet. He flattened himself against the wall beside the door, his Makarov held ready. The humming on the other side of the surprisingly solid planks did not falter. Babcock woke up with a crowing gasp, his eyes wide with shock. John repeated his order and the journalist seemed to be trying to hold his breath.

John's precipitous entry had scattered the rats. Now they returned, scurrying over his boots to get back to their feast. Scott made a sound in the back of his throat, disgust or welcome, John wasn't sure. He took out his knife and began to saw through the ropes binding Babcock's wrists, though all his instincts urged him to go to Scott first. "You speak Russian?" he whispered, pitching his voice a little higher than normal, and Babcock nodded. "Good. I'm Faraz. My friend is outside. We get you away from here, back to Ishkoshim, yes?"

"Oh, God, yes," Babcock muttered.

"If he doesn't understand, you tell him," John went on, jerking his head toward Scott. "Then no more words."

The journalist passed on the message and Scott frowned. "My camera—" he began in English, and Babcock interrupted him almost at once.

"Fuck your camera! You've got more than one and these guys are risking their necks getting us out of here."

"Be quiet!" John ordered, poking Babcock hard between his shoulder blades. He cut the final cord then freed Babcock's ankles before moving on to deal with Scott's bonds. "Now you go." He gestured them toward the window.

Scott didn't hesitate, just made a stirrup of his joined hands and boosted the shorter Babcock up to the sill. The faint scuffles and thumps they made didn't seem to penetrate the door and the iPod's ear buds to alert the guard. Scott didn't need any help snaking through the window, and John followed on his heels. Then they were away, Daryush leading, scrambling up the hillside and over the ridge to where the ponies waited.

With dawn an hour distant, Daryush called a halt. They were far enough into friendly territory now and they could afford to put the last phase of the operation into play.

"Faraz is going back to make sure no one follows us," Daryush said to Babcock, adding more gravel to his voice to disguise it. "We rest the horses for a short while." The wiry beasts didn't need a rest, but Babcock at least did. He'd probably never sat in a saddle in his life.

Without offering any kind of farewell, John reined aside and sent his pony cat-scrambling back the way they'd come. But only far enough to make sure the Americans couldn't hear him make a detour. He would be heading back to the excavation site by a much shorter route, pausing only to leave his mount at the cave for Daryush or Azad to collect later, and change back into his own clothes. With luck he would be able to crawl into his bed just as the sun rose.

* * * *

In the four years he'd been a freelance, Scott had lived through some pretty scary situations. Babcock's translation of Mazdak Rudaki's short *I am handing you over to Shaheen Jalil to give to the Taliban* speech raised the bar to a whole new level. Sitting hogtied in a derelict hovel waiting to be passed across like a birthday present immediately became the front runner in the Crap Your Pants Stakes. The rats just added to the ambience.

Scott had been so pleased to see their

rescuer slide through the window like a ninja snake, he could have kissed the man. Hell, he could have kissed Babcock when the journalist translated the harsh whisper of Russian, telling him they were getting out of there in one piece. The loss of his camera was a minor inconvenience.

The journey back to safety wasn't fun. At first the necessity for silence and stealth meant no talking. By the time they were far enough away from their erstwhile captors to take the risk, Babcock needed all his concentration simply to stay in the saddle. Their unnamed rescuer rode point and Faraz covered their backs, both of them out of conversational range. Besides, Scott soon lost the urge to ask any of the many questions burning on his tongue. He was no stranger to horses, but regardless of his skill level, he hadn't been intimately acquainted with a saddle of any kind for years. The one he currently sat on bore a vague resemblance to a Western rig and should have been comfortable, but his thighs and backside were protesting their unaccustomed positions. Experience told him he'd suffer more in the next few days, even without adding the painful lump on the side of his head and his bruised throat to the quota.

After what seemed an eternity of stumbling around in the slowly lessening dark, they rounded a sharp bend and Scott recognized the outskirts of Ishkoshim just ahead of them. Lights showed in some of the houses. A few people were beginning to stir out of doors; somewhere a car coughed and backfired into life.

Their guide reined in and said something in rapid Russian, pointing across the way.

"He's leaving us here," Babcock croaked and slid off his mount. "Shit!" His legs refused to hold him and he folded to the ground. "Fuck! Scotty, get me up!"

Scott muttered a curse under his breath and dismounted. He staggered when his feet hit the road, but he managed to stay upright. "Thank you," he said earnestly, putting his reins into the Tajik's hand. "I owe you, friend."

The man's quiet chuckle was muffled by the scarf over his mouth, his expression hidden by the fabric and the incongruous night-vision goggles. Scott turned to help Babcock to his feet, and by the time they were both upright, the man and the horses were gone.

"He said the guesthouse is over there," Babcock muttered. "And we should get off the street before an army patrol finds us."

"Sounds good to me," Scott agreed. "C'mon, I need my bed."

"We're not staying."

"But we need to rest. Then we can head

for Khorog and the airport in the morning."

"Fuck that. You think we'll be any safer here or on the road? Just the two of us? No, we're going where we'll have safety in numbers."

"What the hell do you mean?" Scott asked, though he could guess. His stomach sank.

"The dig site. No way is that bastard Mazdak gonna attack so many people just to get us back, not with the army keeping an eye on the place."

"You can't be sure! We could be bringing this shit down on them!"

"Not a chance," Babcock answered scornfully. "Mazdak isn't stupid. Nor is that Shaheen guy."

"And you know this, how? For fuck's sake, Brent! We nearly ended up as an international incident!"

"Exactly. Which is why we're going to

ground with the archaeologists."

"You are insane!" Scott hissed, but he was wasting his breath. "How the hell are we going to convince Mike Preston to let us stay?" Babcock wasn't listening.

"Did you take a good look at those two guys who got us out of there? Night-vision goggles. Who the fuck in this benighted patch of real estate wears night-vision goggles? Not your average Joe. They made damn sure we never saw their faces as well. They gotta be something hush-hush in the Tajik military. There are undercurrents here, Scotty, running deep."

"All the more reason to keep away from the dig. They're archaeologists—students, Brent!"

None of Scott's protests did any good. Babcock didn't stop to clean up and change clothes; he just threw his belongings into his duffel bag. Scott had no choice but to do the same. But as he packed his laptop into his backpack and reached for his toiletries and wash bag, he hesitated, a bottle of cologne in his hand. The Faraz guy who'd climbed into the hut and cut them free... there'd been something familiar about him—

"Get the lead out!" Babcock snapped, sticking his head into Scott's room. "Don't make me wait for you."

"Yes, sir," Scott said shortly.

"Smartass," Babcock responded. Scott bit down on his automatic comeback. The journalist always had to have the last word, and at a time like this Scott would be stupid to start a verbal snipe-fest. Then inspiration struck.

"Hey, Brent, I've got an idea," he said. "How about we wait until the catering guys and the water tankers head out for the site? We'll be more secure in a convoy."

"Now you're using your brain."

Scott was able to retreat to one of the guesthouse's tepid, low-pressured showers, and afterward put on some clean clothes. As he limped out to the 4x4, he felt a little better.

The shower went a short way toward loosening Scott's muscles, but by the time the two men reached the dig and Babcock pulled up beside the site office, his body had started to lock up again. Scott crawled out of the passenger seat, aching in every joint and feeling about ninety years old. His headache increased to blinding proportions, and his stomach reminded him his last proper meal had happened over twenty-four hours ago.

The early morning sun cast long shadows, but they weren't the only ones about. Small groups of students were making for the mess tent, and all Scott wanted to do was join them. A gallon of hot coffee, food, then somewhere to sleep—preferably facedown—jostled for position at the top of his agenda. He managed not to stumble as he trudged toward the mess tent in Babcock's wake, buoyed up by a growing, selfish satisfaction. The journalist was in a worse state than Scott, hobbling like a bowlegged sailor on land for the first time in weeks. He must be chafed and sore as hell. At least Scott didn't have the raw skin.

The half dozen students and couple of lecturers didn't look up as Scott and Babcock entered the tent. John wasn't there, and the disappointment was a punch to Scott's gut. Babcock lurched painfully toward Mike and Anahita, while Scott made a determined beeline to the coffee. He downed the first cup without drawing breath, distantly grateful he didn't scald his throat. The second one he savored, and began to cast his eyes at the various dishes offered for breakfast.

"Holy shit!" someone exclaimed beside him. "What the hell happened to you? You look like a train wreck!" Scott glanced round to see a steadily lengthening line of students gazing at him with concerned expressions.

"Did you get mugged?" another asked. "You should go and see Professor Lane or Doctor Bonneau, they're both paramedics."

"Not mugged," Scott clarified. "Kidnapped."

"*Kidnapped!*" Babcock bellowed at the same time. "For God's sake, those fucking assholes were going to give us to the Taliban! Do you think I was going to stay around waiting for them to make another try to grab me? Grab us? I came here for help and you're going to give it!"

"Uh oh," Scott muttered. Every pair of eyes in the tent focused on the furious journalist.

"In case it escaped your notice,"

Babcock continued with no lessening of volume, "there's no US embassy in that godforsaken dung heap of a village!"

"There isn't one here, either!" Mike retorted loudly, standing to his full height. "I'm not going to allow you to endanger the staff and students under my care. You should have reported what happened to the Army."

"Fuck that! They're probably in on it as well!"

"I doubt it very much. No, Mr Babcock. You and Scott cannot stay here. I'll ask Doctor Bonneau to examine you both, make sure you have no serious injuries, and then you must leave."

Scott abandoned his coffee and hurried across the tent. He grabbed Babcock's wrist as the man clenched his fist and drew back for a swing at the archaeologist. "Thanks, Mike," Scott said quickly. "We'll appreciate the medical check-up. I think I might have a concussion," he lied. Then he wondered if he was lying. The coffee he'd swallowed so quickly began to churn uneasily in his stomach, and his headache rose to new levels of pain.

"I can imagine," Mike said stiffly, then raised his voice again. "Can someone run and ask Doctor Bonneau to come to the site hut?" He met Scott's gaze and relaxed a little. "Come on, I'll take you over there and get you settled. You're looking more than a little green about the gills."

"Yeah," Babcock said unexpectedly. "He tried to fight 'em off and got himself beaten up, choked out. He needs treatment and rest. So do I. Fuck it, we've been tied up without food or water since the night before last, spent hours on horseback, and I'm crippled!"

"Horseback?" Mike's eyebrows rose. By this time they were surrounded by a crowd of avid listeners.

"We were rescued by a couple of Tajiks," Scott answered. Then he began to sweat and saliva filled his mouth. "Uh, I think I'm gonna hurl..." Immediately, supporting arms guided him out of the tent and somehow he managed to hold onto his stomach's contents until they almost reached the site hut. Then, as the final icing on Scott's cake, the military turned up in force. Mike supplied the cherry on top.

"Get Doctor Jones, on the double!" he barked and hauled Scott inside.

# CHAPTER SIX

The roar of engines roused John out of a deep sleep. Those motor sounds did not belong to any of the vehicles which usually came and went from the site. *Military* said his instincts. He rolled out of bed and dressed, ignoring the complaints from muscles long unused to horse riding. Still buttoning his shirt, John left his tent and almost cannoned into Anahita. She clutched his arm, her dark eyes wide and scared. Over by the site hut two military trucks pulled up, and soldiers wearing the distinctive green and yellow camouflage uniforms piled out of them, their guns held ready.

"Scott and Babcock!" she said in a rush. "They were taken by—I don't know who—but they got away and they're here—but the Border Guards have come and Mike wants you."

"Damn! Get all the students into the

mess tent and keep them there. You and Rosie stay with them. Don't run," John added quickly as she turned away. She nodded and walked off briskly, calling to the few postgrads who'd clustered around the door of the hut. They started toward her, and to John's relief the soldiers didn't try to stop them. He, however, was not so lucky. AK47s barred his way when he tried to go inside the hut.

"I can interpret," he said quietly in Russian. "Please let me speak to your officer."

They hesitated only briefly before gesturing him through the door, and he followed the sounds of raised voices to Mike's office. The small room was crowded and the tension hummed like a plucked guitar string. An apparently semiconscious Scott sat slumped in Mike's chair, Yves bent over him shining a penlight in his eyes. In front of the desk, Babcock argued with Mike and a couple of increasingly irritated soldiers, his words a garbled mess of English and Russian.

"Babcock!" Mike bellowed, clearly at the end of his patience. "If you don't shut up and sit down, I'll flatten you myself! John! Thank God you're here. Can you find out what the hell is going on?"

"I'll do my best. Not a word from you, Babcock, until I ask for it." He took a fast glance at the name on the soldier's chest and switched back to Russian. "Sergeant Morovski, I'm fluent—can I help here?" Something like relief crossed the soldiers' faces.

"We received information these two were captured by insurgents," the sergeant said, gesturing to Babcock and Scott. "I want to question them. Do you know them?"

"Yes," he answered. "The older man is Brent Babcock, an American journalist, and the other is Scott Landon, his photographer and also

American. They are following the old Silk Road from Tashkurgan on the Chinese border for a series of articles, probably a book as well. They've visited our excavation site a few times for more material."

"I can speak for myself!" Babcock snarled in Russian.

"I know," John snapped in English. "Just think very carefully about what you say and how you say it."

"Yeah," Scott mumbled. "Honey an' vinegar, Brent."

"What?" Babcock glared as if Scott was speaking in tongues.

"He means," Mike said with angry patience, "don't antagonize the man with the gun."

"I'm not—" he began, then evidently thought better of it and turned to the sergeant. "Sorry," he muttered in Russian. "It's been a difficult time. You want to know what happened, right? We were kidnapped from the Hanis guesthouse in Ishkoshim, pushed into a truck and driven God knows where."

"How many men?"

"Four. All armed to the teeth. Scott tried to fight—got hit on the head and half strangled. We were taken up into the hills," Babcock continued. "To a deserted village. It was dark, but the houses were all ruins as far as I could see. This man—their leader—said he—"

"His name?" Morovski demanded. "Do you know it?"

"Yeah. Mazdak Rudaki. He told us he was going to pass us on to the Taliban."

The soldiers glanced at each other and the sergeant nodded. "You escaped? How?"

"We had help. Two men got us out of there and back to Ishkoshim."

"Their names?" John kept his mask in

place and his muscles did not tense.

"They didn't say," Babcock answered without hesitation and John acknowledged a surge of relief. "I wasn't asking. I figured if they wanted us to know they'd have told us. They weren't with Rudaki, which was good enough for me."

The sergeant nodded again. Both soldiers relaxed slightly and John breathed a little easier.

"John," Mike said, "ask them if they'll escort Scott and Babcock to Khorog,"

"Now hold on—" the journalist started, but John simply talked over him, relaying Mike's question to the sergeant. Morovski shook his head.

"No," he answered. "There's fighting going on between tribal factions, some of them anti-Western. The road to Khorog isn't safe yet. Everyone stays here, where we can protect you."

"But we get supplies ferried in on a regular basis," Mike protested when John translated the reply, "from Khorog as well as Ishkoshim."

"They are not Westerners," the sergeant said calmly. "They are not likely to be attacked."

"Then Landon and Babcock can travel back to Khorog in one of their vehicles," John suggested.

"No. You all stay here."

"For how long?"

"For as long as it takes." Hostility returned to the man's voice. "You all stay here, no one goes through our cordon except the Tajiks working for you."

John glanced at Mike and passed on the instructions. "I don't think we have a choice," he said. "And there isn't a timescale."

Mike's mouth set into a thin line, but he

nodded. "Okay," he agreed. It didn't need translating. With warning glares all round, the sergeant and his sidekick left them to it.

"Suits me just fine," Babcock said triumphantly as soon as the door closed behind the soldiers. "Guess you guys've got a couple of guests for the duration."

"Now that's settled," Yves said before Mike could answer, "these two need to rest. Our tents are nearest, John. Do you mind if Scott crashes in yours?"

Refusal wasn't really possible, though having Scott and the temptation he offered a scant few feet away in the night wasn't on John's list of preferences. "For now," he answered through gritted teeth, "until we can make other arrangements. Are you sure he's okay? He looks pretty rough to me."

"Thanks. Scott isn't concussed, he just drank strong coffee too quickly on an empty stomach. But they're both a little dehydrated. I'll bring over some painkillers and rehydration sachets. He'll need to drink those and plenty of diluted fruit juice. Have you got enough bottles of water?"

"Yes, I think so."

"Good. For now they need a light, high protein meal, fruit juice, and sweetened tea or coffee—not too strong. Then rest."

"Hey," Scott said blearily, "I'm down here, guys. You can talk to me, Doc, I'm not proud."

"Sorry," Yves chuckled. "You go with John, I'll take Babcock. Mess tent, first stop." He ushered Babcock from the room, leaving Mike and John gazing at each other over Scott's head.

"This is not good," the Site Director said.

"Tell me about it. All right, Landon. On

your feet."

"I got stuff in Brent's car," Scott said, wincing as he stood up. John sympathized but didn't let it show.

"It can stay there until we've found somewhere more permanent for you two," Mike answered. "You'll both feel a lot better after a few hours sleep. I'll make an announcement and let everyone get on with what we're here to do. John, can you have a quiet word with the catering staff and see what you can find out about what's going on out there?"

"Will do." John knew exactly what was going on out there; Gulab had done as he had requested and now the tribal leader was moving against Mazdak and probably Shaheen Jalil as well. John hoped his mission hadn't been wrecked, and there was a chance it had been accelerated. With any luck the other leaders would fall in behind Gulab and when the dust finally settled, this part of Tajikistan would stand solidly against extremist incursions.

"I really appreciate this, guys, but can I at least grab my toothbrush?" Scott asked plaintively.

The buzz of speculation in the mess tent immediately fell silent as the five men entered. Mike made his announcement while John and Yves ushered their temporary charges to the long food counter. John quietly explained the situation to the Tajiks doing the cooking and serving, and noted their lack of surprise. With Babcock listening in, he didn't ask questions.

Yves recommended the scrambled eggs and the pancakes oozing with honey. John selected his own choice of breakfast and took over a nearby table. Scott sat carefully in the chair beside him, groaning as his backside hit the seat.

"I'm a disgrace to Texas," the photographer muttered. "Okay, I haven't sat on a horse for five, maybe six years, but it's no excuse." Scott was pale under his tan, his eyes heavy-lidded and dark-ringed in their sockets. Red-gold stubble shadowed his jaw and his hair was a tangled mess. John wanted to put his arms around him and— He stopped the impulse in its tracks.

"You'll live," he said crisply. "Eat slowly. Overload your stomach too quickly and the food will bounce right back up."

"Okay, Dad." The accompanying grin had become familiar, even in so short a time: pure Scott, irritatingly cocky and cheerful. Not at all endearing.

"Don't push your luck," John warned, and managed to keep his own smile hidden.

"Be gentle with me, I'm a sick man."

John treated that with the contempt it

deserved.

On the other side of the table Yves was getting a blow by blow account of their ordeal from Babcock whether he wanted it or not. It began with their capture in the guesthouse, and a widening audience hung on every word.

"Are you ready to get out of here?" John asked in a low voice.

"God, yes," Scott answered equally quietly. "Brent generates enough hot air to power a small nation, and I gotta tell you, man, it didn't happen the way he's saying."

"No?"

"No." But Scott didn't elaborate until he'd retrieved his backpack from the 4x4 and they were heading toward John's tent. Then, "Brent picked up a lead on a story," he said abruptly. "He'd arranged to meet with Mazdak and interview him. We met his men outside the guesthouse and they drove us to the abandoned village. They jumped us when we got there. Mazdak planned on handing us over to another chief, one involved with the Taliban." He paused to yawn. "I had a hunch it wasn't like it seemed but Brent didn't want to know. We were lucky to escape."

"Yes," John said.

"Brent thinks the guys who rescued us were Tajik Special Forces. That's why he kept quiet about the one name we knew."

"It's possible, I suppose. If this Mazdak is a known troublemaker, they're probably watching him."

"Yeah." Scott yawned again. "God, I feel like a zombie."

"There is a vague resemblance," John drawled.

"Bastard," Scott mumbled. "See how you'd feel if—" Another yawn interrupted him.

"Just try to stay on your feet for a little

while longer." John opened the door of his tent and ushered him inside, unzipped the bedroom flap as well. "Crash," he ordered.

"Yeah. Thanks, Doc." Scott shambled past him and sat on the camp bed. He pawed the sleeping bag out of the way and just sagged facedown on the narrow mattress. His eyes closed even as his head hit the pillow. John turned away then stopped. Muttering under his breath he crossed the bedroom in a few strides and lifted Scott's legs onto the bed, pulled off his boots, and draped the sleeping bag over his shoulders. Scott didn't move.

He should have looked defenseless, lying there unshaven and exhausted. He didn't. All John could see of his profile revealed Scott's character in the stubborn jaw and generous mouth. Not a youth's face, but the features of an adult, strong and determined even in sleep. Something poignant and bittersweet clenched around his heart. Not for the first time, John acknowledged the essential loneliness of his chosen career, the lack of a settled home base and someone to share it. Now Scott Landon had strolled into his life and all Scott wanted from him was casual, no-strings sex. It would be too easy to forget all the reasons why he should stay away; his mission—hell, his job with MI6 and all it entailed—their age difference. Before he realized what he was doing, John stroked the untidy blond hair. His fingers caught on a silky tangle, but the sleeping man didn't flinch.

"Damn you," John whispered painfully, and hurried from his tent.

* * * *

Finally horizontal, Scott relaxed with a long shuddering sigh of relief. The pallet on the narrow bed was firm but comfortable, and the pillow sheer bliss. He was vaguely aware the pillow smelled like John, of dust and sun and *Element* cologne, with a hint of smoke from the brazier sitting outside the mess tent. He hadn't slept for over thirty-six hours and now he slid into sleep like a seal into water, while someone—John—settled the covers over him.

Exhausted though he was, his aches dulled by painkillers and anti-inflammatories, Scott did not have a restful sleep. The images of his laughing, mocking captors, the threats Babcock—the asshole—translated with painstaking detail, even the fucking rats, combined to haunt his dreams with nightmare scenarios. Yet every time they jolted him half awake, he'd hug the pillow a little closer and a primal sensory perception told him he was safe, letting him sink back into slumber.

Eventually Scott rose through layers of consciousness to the realization he was thirsty, hungry, and somewhere safe and secure. His muscles were stiff, his wrists and ankles sore from the ropes, and the knot on the left side of his head throbbed, but it all paled to insignificance. He was in John's bed, if not in the way he'd hoped and still planned. He turned his face into the pillow and breathed in a deep lungful of John-scented air. *Hugo Element* and smoke and—*a dark figure pressing close, cutting his painfully tight bonds, then gesturing him toward a glassless window and the promise of escape. Night-goggles and a scarf pulled so high no sign of his features showed at all...* The flash of recall stunned Scott for a moment. Then he shook his head to clear it, wincing when his muscles protested the movement, and decided he should join the rest of the world.

Slowly Scott forced his eyes open. The tent was full of shadows, so he must have slept the day away. He managed to find the will to swing his legs off the bed and sat up, groaning. He desperately wanted a long soak in a hot tub, preferably with whirlpool action. And a massage. But even more he wanted something to eat, and to drink the gallon of coffee he'd promised himself. Maybe then he'd be able to connect the dots currently racketing around in his aching head.

When he yawned his way into the main compartment of the tent, Scott found a note, a bottle of fruit juice, and some pills waiting for him on the table. *Drink all this and take the tablets.*

"Huh!" Scott snorted, but obeyed. The liquid felt and tasted wonderful as it slid down his throat. It reminded his stomach it wanted something more substantial.

Cautiously Scott stretched his muscles. All things considered, he'd come through the whole scary experience in pretty good shape.

All he needed now was food. And answers; some of those dots were beginning to fall into line, making an interesting picture. But not one he could discuss with Babcock.

First things first. Right then, Scott's top priority centered on his belly, fuelled by the scent of food wafting over the tent village. He headed for the mess at a fast clip, spurred on by the rumblings in his stomach. The place was crowded, and he joined the queue for food to the accompaniment of a gratifying number of concerned queries. The excitement of the morning had mostly died down. Now the general chatter was about the much older levels being uncovered in some of the trenches.

Scott looked around but couldn't see Babcock anywhere, and breathed a sigh of relief. John, though, was in a huddle with Mike and Yves over in a corner, so when he'd been served, Scott carried his tray to their table.

"Can I join y'all?" he asked, and received two smiles and a frown.

"Of course," Mike answered. "We were just discussing you and Babcock."

Scott took the seat next to Yves. "Uh, okay?" he said cautiously.

"Yes. We've partially solved the housing issue. Rosie and Anahita have agreed to double up, leaving Rosie's tent for Babcock. But he won't share. Which leaves us with a slight problem. You."

"Oh. Uh, I'll share with anyone." Scott kept his earnest gaze on Mike's face, not daring to glance at John. "Hell, give me some blankets and I'll bed down here or in the site hut. Whichever suits y'all best."

"Well," Mike began, "here and the huts are out of the question. My tent doubles as an overflow from my office in the hut, and Yves's doubles as the Medical Center." He hesitated, then, "John? Won't you reconsider?"

"All right. He can stay with me." To say his agreement was grudging would be an understatement. "There's enough room for a pallet in the living compartment. But if he snores, he's out. He can sleep in their car."

"Thanks, John," Mike said earnestly. "I appreciate this."

"So do I," Scott said, keeping his elation under wraps. This was almost too good to be true and he wondered if he could successfully fake sleepwalking. "And I don't snore. You won't hear a thing from me, honest."

"Good," John said and stood. "I'll go and see what bedding I can scrounge." He strode out of the tent with an air of determination.

"John can be a bit abrasive sometimes," Mike said, his smile rueful. "But he's okay." That, Scott assumed, was an accolade in the peculiarly British, understated way.

"Yeah," he agreed soberly. "I guess the military's presence is gonna cause some problems?"

"No reason why it should," Yves replied. "We rarely go into the village in any case, and any souvenirs we wanted, we've already bought."

"I've contacted the University in Dushanbe," Mike continued. "They're getting in touch with the local commander to keep up with the situation. If there's any overt danger, we'll be evacuated."

"But we're hoping and praying it won't happen," Yves said. "This site is proving to be very interesting. John thinks Anahita's found what can best be described as a post office."

"What?" Scott smiled. "You're kidding me."

"No, not at all." Yves chuckled. "He's translated lists, instructions to buy and sell, letters to business partners, stewards, families. We think they were stored there to be taken on by whichever caravans were traveling in the right direction. He and Anahita are very excited about it."

"Wow. That's pretty cool. Hey, *mi Capitán*, can I get some photos of them?"

"Don't see why not," Mike replied. "Talk to John. He'll sort out the most interesting for you."

The two archaeologists stayed with him while he finished his meal, answering his questions with relaxed candidness until Babcock turned up.

# CHAPTER SEVEN

As soon as he returned to his tent, John dropped Scott's bedding on the floor, zipped the tent door closed, and took out his satphone to contact Maria. Azad had helped him locate the spare pallet, blankets, and pillow, and in the process updated him on what was going on up in the hills. Gulab was mopping up Mazdak and taking on Shaheen, and so far Gulab had the upper hand.

The situation report didn't take long, and Maria confirmed that official and unofficial plans were in hand to expedite the evacuation of the archaeologists, possibly with United Nations' help. He'd pass along some of the information to Mike in the morning.

John hid the satphone and opened the door flap before typing up his notes on his borrowed laptop, so when Scott returned he rightly took it as an invitation to enter.

"Hey," said Scott, dropping into the canvas chair beside him. John looked up, dragging his attention back to the twenty-first century.

"Hullo," he said. "How are you feeling now?"

"I'm fine. Still a bit stiff and sore, but it'll pass. Brent's working on the epic report he's going to be selling to the highest bidder as soon as he can. Me, I'm pretty pissed about my camera."

"What about it?" John asked.

"Mazdak's gang still has it. Luckily there were only a few pictures on it, so it's no real loss as far as shots are concerned. But it's a good camera, hard to replace until I get back to civilization."

"But not the only one you have."

"Hell, no."

"You were bloody lucky to get out of there in one piece."

"Yeah, and the rats were kinda gross. A couple of bruises and some rope burns, is all." He shot John a sideways glance, his smile widening. "No saddle sores, either. Ah'm a Texas boy, remember." He paused, his gaze moving appreciatively over John's body. "I can ride anything."

John sighed. It wasn't the most blatant pick-up line Scott offered him, but it was close. "Why aren't I surprised?" he answered caustically, refusing to acknowledge that the roughened drawl affected him in any way. "How are you and Babcock doing on this whole Silk Road odyssey?"

"Pretty good. He's only got a couple more places left on his list, and then the hard work starts."

"The—?"

"Yeah. He writes the damn book and haggles with me over the photos. But to hell with that. We need to talk."

"Um, we are. You're flapping your jaw, making noises, which counts as talking in my book."

"Smartass. Tell me about Faraz."

"Who?" John kept his expression one of mild puzzlement with a conscious effort. "As far as I know we don't have a Faraz on the catering or supply teams. Unless he's one of the part-time drivers?"

"Don't play dumb. But maybe we shouldn't be having this conversation here. How about we turn it into pillow-talk?"

"How about we don't." John fixed him with a steely glare. "I don't play games, Landon, and I don't fuck around. So get over yourself and leave me alone."

Scott's grin bloomed white and wide.

"Hey, I just want to talk, y'know? And thank one of the guys who hauled our asses out of the fire last night. Or this morning. Hell, he saved my life. Both our lives."

A chill knotted tight in John's belly. "Well, since I have no idea who this Faraz is," he snapped, "I'm unable to pass on your message."

"You certain? Damn, but you surely have the playing-hard-to-get card down pat." He turned soulful eyes on John and leaned a little closer. "Okay, forget Faraz and the fact he's the same height as you, has the same set to his shoulders, and the same way of canting his head a little to the right when he's thinking—and the fact I was pretty damn sure I could smell a vague hint of *Hugo Element* underneath the horse, sweat, and wood smoke. Which, by coincidence, you're wearing now. *Element*, that is, not the—"

"Is there a point to this ramble?" John interrupted, edging back in his chair.

"Yeah. Y'see, it's a well known and documented fact, after a life-threatening experience the survivors have this primal urge to indulge in life-affirming sex. No way am I going to jump Brent's bones, and college geeks don't do it for me. Professors, on the other hand, or guys with doctorates... Am I unsubtle enough for you, Doc?" His smiling mouth was a study in sensuality, and John's blood caught fire. But he would not give in to the demands of his body.

"You are a feckless idiot!" he snapped, trapped where he sat. As usual, the insults didn't affect Scott, except to make his smile wider.

"Yup. That's me. Totally without feck. Had it surgically removed when I was a little kid. Along with my foreskin. Wanna see?"

"No. When will you get it into your head

I am not interested—"

"John," Scott said, all banter gone now. "I kissed you. You kissed me back. I think we both know where this is going. So how about it? No strings, no commitment, just two adults fucking each other. That's all. Who the hell is gonna know? It stays in here, between us and no one else." His voice developed a telling huskiness, the blue of his eyes drowning in the black of his expanded pupils.

Desire hit John like a juggernaut. His blood flowed hot through his veins, filling his groin with a heavy heat, and he didn't immediately recognize the emotion behind Scott's blatant lust. When he did, it tempered his reaction. Whether Scott knew it or not, he needed something more than sex from John; he needed the simple, uncomplicated reassurance of human contact.

John found himself in a dilemma; should

he provide it? His mission wouldn't be affected. Gulab Turi was moving against the Taliban sympathizers, which MI6 wanted—as long as Gulab came out victorious. But what of the cost to himself? It had been a long time since he'd found himself drawn to someone as strongly as he was to the younger man. The much younger man, and all the perfectly valid reasons to keep his distance were still in play. Then he discovered he'd spent too long thinking.

Scott made his move, placing his hands on John's shoulders and leaning close to plant an open-mouthed, tongue-probing kiss like the one he'd stolen a few days before. John could taste Scott's desperation and that decided everything as far as he was concerned. He shoved hard at Scott, sending him rocking back in his chair.

"You," John said sternly, "are an impatient oaf with as much finesse as a bull on a ski slope." He closed his laptop and stood to turn off the single light bulb above the desk, all the while sensing the storm of emotion emanating from Scott. Enough illumination filtered through the blue nylon walls to show him Scott's startled disappointment. John glanced swiftly around, then back at Scott. "This is a tent, remember? Interior lighting? Shadows on the wall—understand?" Scott gazed at him uncomprehendingly for a moment, obviously attempting to process the words then nodded jerkily. Two long steps put John right inside Scott's personal space, looming over the seated man. "Nor is it soundproof, so you will keep your voice down." As if to underline the point, Yves and Mike could be heard outside, talking in front of Mike's tent. "How quiet can you be, Scott?"

Hope brightened in Scott's eyes. "Very, very qui—" John bent down and claimed his mouth, silencing him. At once Scott's arms snaked around his ribs and locked tight, and when John straightened, Scott rose as well, molded to him but trying to get even closer. The unspoken demand for more removed the last thread of separation between them.

John wedged his leg between Scott's thighs, slid one hand to the silky hair at the back of his neck and the other down his spine to his buttocks. Scott tried to arch his back and force himself even closer, and would have groaned aloud if John hadn't compelled him forward and covered his mouth again. It didn't stop him riding John's thigh, his erection grinding against John's hip.

"Slow down," John whispered against his throat. "There's no rush."

"Can't," Scott gasped. "Need this, John. God! Need to feel—" He was out of control and John's was slipping fast.

"All right. Come on, then. We'll get you

there," he whispered between nip-sharpened kisses to Scott's chin and throat. Scott's arms were clamped around him in a bruising death grip, but John managed to push him back far enough to unfasten the button and zipper of Scott's jeans. He freed Scott's cock from his damp cotton boxers and closed his hand firmly around the heated, wet flesh. A strangled growl escaped from the back of Scott's throat and his hips jerked desperately. John kissed him again, gagging him with his mouth, working his hand in swift, twisting pumps. Scott writhed, rutting against him, his nails digging into John's shoulder blades, and John kissed his way along Scott's stubbled jaw to his throat.

"Shit!" Scott whispered. "I've wanted this—wanted you—know what I was thinkin', hogtied in that fuckin' hovel? I—God, I love your mouth—was gonna die an' all I had from you was one kiss. Yes, there! Kept on—oh, fuck, don't stop—thinkin' one more kiss an'—you might have—was too shit-scared to pop a boner, but—oh, God—" He broke off with a stifled moan as John pressed his fingers between Scott's ass cheeks, seeking the entrance to his body. He traced over the quivering muscle before sliding his hand farther to the smooth, sensitive skin behind Scott's balls.

"Don't you ever shut up?" John murmured and gently scraped his perineum with a blunt fingernail. Scott convulsed, spurting hot and slick over John's hand and his own belly, his mouth wide in a silent shout of ecstasy.

John gentled him through the orgasm and its aftershocks, until Scott was a semi-comatose weight hanging in his embrace and he could steer them both to lie on the pallet.

"Jesus," Scott muttered weakly. "I think my brains just came out my dick."

John smiled. "I won't state the obvious."

His own cock was painfully erect, constricted in his clothing, but he could wait.

"Haven't come like that for..." He sounded drunk, high on pleasure. "For years. If ever." He fumbled for John's fly. "C'n feel how hard you are. Your turn, Doc."

"Think you'll be able to stay awake long enough?"

"Oh, yeah."

"Good. Because I have plans for you, Scott Landon."

"Yeeaah?" It was a drawled, heavy-eyed, smirking challenge. "If you mean what I think you mean, bring it."

Scott didn't particularly want to let go of him, but clothing needed to be removed and he didn't know how long this compliant John would stay around. His nerve endings were tingling, his whole body felt heavy and light at the same time, still flying on the endorphins.

"Life-affirming sex," he slurred giddily. "Gotta love it. C'mon, get naked. I wanna see you." Though that held an element of wishful thinking to it, he admitted regretfully. The gloom within the tent meant John was nothing but shadow and strange highlights. Come sunrise, though, there'd be light enough for Scott to view all of him. And explore.

He reached up and traced the curve of John's mouth, feeling rather than seeing the smile growing under the light contact. He'd already learned when John wasn't irritated, his mouth had a natural smiling tilt and an interesting fullness to his lower lip. And if kissing was an Olympic event, he was gold medal material. Most of the time Scott and his hookups didn't bother overmuch with the preliminaries; now he realized he could have been missing out on some good stuff. Then again, it might only be because John possessed a rare and addictive talent. If it was, then Scott owed it to himself to get as much of it as he could before they parted company.

"Condoms and lube," John murmured. "I hope you have some, because I don't."

"Wash bag," he answered quickly. "And why aren't you naked yet?" He shed his T-shirt as fast as he could, and shimmied out of his jeans and boxers. Then he used his shirt to wipe the drying semen from his belly and lay back on the pallet, hands behind his head, waiting for John to search through his backpack for the bag and its vital contents. At last they were found and tossed onto his chest. The plastic bottle was cold on his heated skin and he stifled a yelp of surprise. "Jerk," he muttered, grinning.

"So warm it before I use it on you," John said, and stripped off his own clothes. Scott watched avidly, wishing the tent wasn't so dark.

All he could see were tantalizing glimpses of long limbs, the lines of a lean torso, and the denser shadow of hair across John's chest and at his crotch. It was enough to show him John had the sinewy body of a long distance runner, strength and endurance implicit in every economical movement. No way was it an old man's body, and Scott couldn't understand why John was fixated on the difference in their ages. The man was hot, end of story.

His uncut cock jutting proudly from its bed of black curls, John knelt beside the pallet and leaned down to take Scott's mouth in a gentle, exploring kiss. His tongue drifted over Scott's lips, slipped inside to start a slow dance with Scott's and turn his bones to liquid. John's was a different kind of hunger, it seemed—not a starving man seizing what food he could, but a gourmet at a feast, a slow savoring of all Scott was offering.

"I won't flatter your already inflated ego by telling you how handsome you are," he whispered into Scott's ear. His voice was rich velvet and honeyed sin, holding Scott in thrall as surely as ropes of silk. "How I wish I could spread you out on cushions and lie with you all day. You're made for sunlight." He trailed kisses across Scott's shoulder, then back along his clavicle to the shallow dip where the two bones met.

Somehow Scott found the coordination to caress his fingers through John's hair as John cat-lapped and kissed his way down Scott's breastbone.

"Fuck, yes," Scott gasped. "Sun—you—we could—" John's mouth closed over his nipple and his spine arched. He needed to shout, needed to be quiet, needed *more*, and the conflicting impulses added to the spiraling lust burning in his blood. "God, your mouth is—"

"At least I've discovered a way to shut you up," John drawled softly, his lips moving warm and smooth on Scott's skin.

"Hah. You could recite the Yellow Pages and I think I'd get off on it," he muttered breathlessly. "Just don't stop."

John's hand ghosted down his chest, leaving a trail of sparking nerve endings in its wake, and spread out on his belly, the weight of his palm and splayed fingers providing a much needed anchor to reality. Even so, Scott couldn't help his instinctive buck into the possessive pressure. John chuckled and stretched out beside him. There wasn't room on the narrow pallet for both of them and the floor was just a groundsheet over hard dirt, but John didn't seem bothered. He slid down Scott's body and proceeded to explore every inch he could reach with mouth and tongue and careful teeth. He was in no hurry, and Scott gradually lost track of time, of the here and now. He soared higher, aware only of the rich pleasure each caress brought, discovering his own body's responses to levels he'd never experienced before.

Then John's tongue circled his navel and Scott bit back a moan. The head of his semi-hard cock brushed John's cheek, the abrasiveness of stubble almost a sensation overload on the very edge of painful. But in a very good way—and then John just turned his head and closed his mouth around the wet glans.

"Yes!" Scott hissed. "There! That's what I want!" John chuckled, the vibration doing sinful things to Scott's over sensitized flesh. Scott felt John's tongue flicker-slide over the slit, probe delicately into it, and for a moment he couldn't breathe.

It was too much, too intense, not a simple fuck at all. And somewhere in the delirium of ecstasy it occurred to Scott that John was making love to him, cherishing him. The thought was lost the second he heard the click of the bottle being flipped open. The cool lotion being smoothed over his perineum and worked into his body's entrance completed the memory-wipe. The remorseless sucking coaxed his cock fully erect, his ball sac to gather up, and Scott barely registered the clever fingers opening him, stretching him. When John lifted his head, letting Scott's cock slap back onto his belly, Scott moaned aloud.

  "Shh," John whispered. "Open your legs."

  Scott obeyed with commendable swiftness, raising his knees and spreading himself wide, ignoring his protesting muscles. John moved to kneel between his thighs. Scott canted his hips just so, and watched avidly as John rolled a condom onto his own cock.

  "Hurry it up!" he pleaded. "I'm desperate

here!"

"Really? I'd never have guessed."

"Smarta—" Scott broke off with a groan of delight as John guided his cock to his entrance and eased inside. "Oh, feels so good..." And it did. The hard length slowly sank into him, and he relished the heated fullness, welcomed it. He wrapped his arms around John's shoulders, then curled his spine, clamped his knees high up on John's ribs, and locked his ankles over his buttocks. "Okay, stud. Give it to me."

So John did, but not in the way Scott expected. Instead of a fast, hard fucking, John moved in long, slow thrusts, lifting Scott on a rising spiral of sensual overload. When the strokes began to slide over his prostate, Scott knew he couldn't last much longer. As if he'd read Scott's mind, John upped the pace, hips plunging his cock deep into Scott at every thrust. This time, when Scott climaxed, he would have shouted his release if John hadn't smothered him with his mouth again. Two more powerful drives and John lost his rhythm, his body spasming into orgasm before slumping onto Scott.

"Holy fucking God..." Scott burbled deliriously, already more than half comatose. "We have so got to do this again."

"In your dreams," John whispered as he carefully withdrew. Scott muttered a protest when John managed to free himself from Scott's determined octopus hold, but he shut up at once when John kissed him.

By the time John disposed of the condom and used Scott's T-shirt to clean them both, the younger man was on the verge of sleep. The sensible thing would be for John to leave him to sleep it off and go to his own bed, but he didn't. He dragged his own mattress, pillow, and sleeping bag off the camp bed and dropped them alongside Scott. Then he rolled Scott on his side, settled himself on the pallet, and gathered him back into his arms. With a pleased mumble, Scott burrowed his face into John's neck, wrapped arms and legs around him, and relaxed into deeper slumber.

"Idiot," John whispered and pressed a gentle kiss to the blond head on his shoulder, then pulled the sleeping bag over them both.

John doubted he'd get much rest, and he was right. Scott dreamed, and by his restless mutterings about rifles and Taliban and rats, they were not good dreams. Each time, John soothed him with caresses and reassuring whispers, and each time Scott wormed closer, seeking the solace of his embrace. He was a heavy weight in John's arms, sweaty and stubble-jawed, but John did not relinquish his hold in the slightest. If it was humanly possible, he'd make sure Scott spent a lot more time sleeping in his bed. But it could be nothing but a pleasant fantasy.

Not long after dawn, Scott yawned and stretched, froze for a few seconds, then whispered, "John?"

"Who were you expecting?"

"No one. Wondered if I was having a better dream." He yawned again, licked at the pulse in John's throat, and kissed the place. "Uh, did I keep you awake? I kinda remember some nightmares..."

"Not really. Was that the first time you've been in a difficult situation?"

Scott smothered his laughter in John's shoulder. "You and your understatements. Nah. My last big job in Peru got a little crazy. Felipe was hunting out lost cities and lost tribes and I took the photos for him. We were hit by storms, treed by a herd of wild pigs—God, they scared the shit out of me—nearly capsized by the biggest caiman I ever saw, and the spiders. You wouldn't believe the size of those freakin' things!"

"And before?"

"First, white water rafting in New Zealand for a company specializing in extreme sports, and a couple of months with Jodi Guildenstern, covering the Pakistani floods. It was scary at times but Jodi held my hand." He smiled fondly. "She's a good friend."

"I'm sure," he said quietly. No matter how dangerous the situations Scott had found himself in, John would be prepared to bet serious money he had never been faced with losing his life at the hands of another human being. That brought a whole new level of terror into play, as John knew from his own first encounter with someone trying to kill him. Scott's almost silent laughter faded away and his arms tightened around John's ribs. It didn't take much intuition for John to guess Scott's thoughts had strayed to the same place. "So where do you go after the Silk Road?" he asked as a distraction ploy.

"Jodi wants me to go to Darfur with her."

It was John's turn to tighten his hold. "Not exactly a bed of roses," he murmured.

"No, but after Mazdak's fun-fest, I'm pretty sure I can handle most things life throws at me."

"Yes," John said.

"So, uh, where do you go after this?"

"Back home initially. Afterward, who knows? It depends on what my agent finds for me."

"Africa, maybe?"

"I very much doubt it. African languages and history aren't my specialty."

"Where's home?"

"London."

Scott propped himself up on one elbow, peering down at him. His hair was a tangled mess, the blondness taking on strange tints in the blued light filtering through the tent. His eyes were heavy-lidded with sleepy desire, and his slightly swollen mouth wore its usual jaunty smile. "London's a big place."

"Finchley." John rented a second floor bed-sit not far from the Underground station. If he managed to spend more than a few months there in any given year, he considered himself lucky.

"Oh." Scott said, clearly having no idea where Finchley was, other than near London. John didn't elaborate. Instead he craned up and kissed him.

"Good morning," he said belatedly. "I'm off to the ablutions. I'll bring back coffee if the caterers turn up by the time I'm done."

## CHAPTER EIGHT

The pallets weren't so comfortable with John gone. Scott shifted around restlessly for a while, half listening to the snores coming from the next tent and relishing his body's aches. Not all of them came from his kidnap and rescue. He wondered briefly if the faint noises they'd made last night had been overheard, and thought probably not. John had been very insistent on silence, or at least as quiet as they could manage.

Scott's smile widened to a grin and he squirmed happily, still feeling the satisfying fullness of John's cock in him. He didn't often play catcher, but for John he'd make an exception. Somehow the man found all his buttons and played him like a maestro. He wished they could have a lot more time together, time when they wouldn't have to worry about being heard and could make as much noise as necessary. His grin faltered and faded when he remembered it wasn't going to happen. In a matter of days they'd be going their separate ways. But they'd have the nights for as long as it took the intertribal fighting to fizzle out, and Scott fully intended to make the most of them.

He rolled over and wrapped his arms around the pillow, planting his face in it and taking in the mixture of scents which said *John* to his conscious and subconscious brain. Images flickered across his closed eyelids: the way John's mouth became sculpted sensuality when it wasn't thinned to an angry or disapproving line; the way the lines at the corners of his eyes crinkled when he smiled his often wry smile; and his eyes, so deep and dark and sometimes oddly gentle—the way John soothed him when he'd half woken from nightmares. Then Scott saw again the dimly lit interior of the hut and heard the harsh whisper of incomprehensible Russian. He felt the rock-steady strength of the stranger as he leaned close to sever Scott's bonds, and smelled the unmistakable thread of *Element* beneath the odors of horse and smoke and sweat.

Faraz. Who shared more than a few similarities with John. Babcock had been so sure their rescuers were Tajik Special Forces, but John was an academic, an archaeologist. No way could anyone fake his depth of knowledge and love for his chosen career. Yet at the same time Scott found it hard to believe the *Hugo* franchise had a foothold in this part of Tajikistan.

Next door, Mike stopped snoring. The level of light slowly increased and soon more people would be stirring. John would be back from his visit to the latrines. Then the sound of engines heralded the arrival of the catering crew, and with them the promise of coffee. Quickly Scott rolled out of bed and stood up, ignoring the twinges from overused thigh muscles. He rooted out a moderately clean pair of jeans from his duffel and pulled them on, not bothering with boxers. He needed to at least attempt to solve the Faraz/John mystery before it drove him crazy, but he wasn't sure where to start.

There were papers and notebooks sorted neatly on the makeshift desk, and they seemed to be his logical first choice. But it didn't take long for Scott to realize every one was excavation notes or transcriptions and speculative comments on both. They told him John was a consummate professional with a hell of a way with words, but he already knew that.

*If John helped in the rescue, why was he keeping it hidden? Why masquerade as Faraz? John was sexy as hell, but he was no James*

*Bond. Was he? How the hell could he be? He was the Assistant Site Director for God's sake!* Voices outside interrupted his thoughts: John and Mike exchanging friendly banter. They reminded Scott appearances needed to be kept up, and the tent smelled of sex. He hurriedly returned John's bedding to the sleeping compartment then squirted a few sprays of deodorant in the air and on his body. When John entered the tent a few moments later, Scott was tugging a clean T-shirt over his head.

The day was—odd. Scott hauled buckets, pushed wheelbarrows, delivered water bottles around the excavations, and caught only glimpses of John. In between the grunt work, he took photos of everything he could get away with. Including some of the oblivious John and the shots Babcock wanted of the armed-to-the-teeth Border Patrol standing watch over the diggers. But there was no mistaking the underlying tension pervading the site. Everyone seemed jumpy, apart from Mike and John. They were oases of calm, spreading reassurance about them on their more frequent than usual patrols of the trenches.

When a series of faint pops rattled away in the distance, none of the postgrads in the mosque trench spoke or moved for at least a breath-held minute.

"*Sons comme des fusils,*" Jacques muttered nervously, glancing nervously around at his fellow students, and Scott could make a good guess at the translation. Gunfire.

"Yeah," he said. Nobody else said anything.

Babcock arrived at a fast walk, red-faced and sweating, a fiercely determined light in his eyes. "Scotty, quit hauling crap and come on. There's a firefight happening out there—"

John appeared at his shoulder, as cool and unruffled as the journalist was disheveled. "And what, exactly, do you intend to do about it?" he asked with deceptive mildness.

"Do? My job, of course. C'mon, Scotty, haul ass!"

"By that," John said, shooting a swift glare at Scott and stopping him in his tracks, "I assume you intend to go up into the hills and photograph the action?" The words were bitten out with acidic coldness and Scott flinched. John was annoyed. No, John was out and out furious.

"Got it in one, Doc. It's what I do. C'mon, Scott."

"No." John said flatly. "In the unlikely event you get past Sergeant Morovski's cordon, your presence out there will almost inevitably draw fire on us. Those soldiers are there for a reason. Under other circumstances, I would have no problem with you going out to commit virtual suicide, but these postgraduate students are in my care and I will not allow you to endanger them. So, no, Mr Babcock. You and Mr Landon are remaining here."

"The hell we are! You don't get to tell me what I can and can't do! Out of my way!"

If it wasn't so serious, Scott might have found it amusing, watching the short, stocky, bulldog of a man facing up to the taller, lighter-built archaeologist. He certainly found it hot. John was neither domineering nor aggressive, but his cold, calm assumption of authority was one hell of a turn on. Unexpectedly so. Scott shifted cautiously, attempting to relieve some of the pressure on his cock. There was no protecting cotton between his flesh and the zipper. "Brent, he has a point," he said quietly. "These kids—"

"Are their concern, not mine! There's a

story out there and we're getting it!" Fists clenched, Babcock strode forward, clearly intending to barrel right through John. A blur of action, a yelp of pain and shock, and Babcock was bent over, one arm extended behind him, his hand imprisoned, the limb twisted against its joints. John held him there without obvious effort.

"That firefight is your doing," John said coldly. "If you hadn't started asking questions, poking around, people wouldn't be dying out there. They will not be dying in here. You are staying put if I have to chain you to a rock. Do you understand me, Mr Babcock?"

"Fuck you!" But he'd capitulated and everyone knew it. John released him from the hold and Babcock stepped away from him, rubbing his wrist and glowering. Then Scott found himself held by John's cold, dark gaze and he swallowed convulsively.

"Do you have a problem with this, Mr Landon?"

"No. None at all," he said quickly. "Brent, he's right. We can choose whether or not to risk our lives, but we can't put others in danger in the process." Babcock sneered but didn't speak.

\* \* \* \*

"What was all that about?" Mike demanded when John joined him outside the site hut. "Thought you were going to twist Babcock's arm off for a moment. The kids were fascinated," he added with a smile.

"He was all set to try for Journalist of the Year by documenting the small war out there."

"Thought it might be." Mike shook his head. "The man's a menace. At least Scott is making himself useful." They both turned to gaze out to the hills as another burst of gunfire crackled in the distance. Then a single, larger bang awoke faraway echoes. "What the hell?"

"Sounded like a mortar shell," John said, a twist of anxiety under his ribs.

"Oh, shit. We're sitting ducks, aren't we?"

John nodded. "If they come closer, I'm afraid so."

"Only about half of the caterers turned up this morning," Mike said abruptly. "Can't say I blame them. I've been on to Dushanbe University and apparently the UN is offering help in getting us out. The Tajik generals aren't so keen."

"It could take a while," John agreed with a placidity he didn't feel.

"But it is going to happen." Mike's optimism didn't waver. "There are kids of half a dozen different nationalities here. The government won't risk a major international incident."

"They'll do their damnedest to avoid it," John agreed, and didn't add that the same circumstance made them a prime target for the anti-government insurgents if they broke through the lines.

"So we can't leave the site open like this," Mike continued. "We should start packing the finds and backfilling the more vulnerable trenches."

"A good plan," John answered. "It'll give the students something positive to do as well."

"Exactly. Would you have a chat with the sergeant? Tell him what we're doing and find out if he has any up-to-date news on the evacuation."

"Will do."

Sergeant Morovski knew nothing more than John—less, in fact, and John didn't enlighten him. The man started to dig in his heels on evacuating the boxed finds as well as the archaeologists, but John's impassioned speech on the wealth of Tajik history and the sergeant's own legacy as a Tajik persuaded him the effort should be made. Moderately satisfied, John returned to the dig.

The first trenches to be made secure were the mosque and Anahita's 'post office'. Polythene sheets covered the cleared surfaces, and the soil carefully spread over them. The work went quickly and by the end of the day both trenches were filled and leveled off.

When everyone, including Babcock, congregated in the mess tent for the evening meal, the mood was subdued at first but reasonably relaxed. The contents of the site hut were safely packed away, and only the less vulnerable levels waited to be backfilled. No more gunfire echoed in the hills and the journalist seemed to be over his surliness, though he aimed too many jibes at Scott, in John's opinion.

Scott, on the other hand, rapidly became the life and soul of the party. His jaunty cheerfulness and tall tales from his rainforest experience started most of them laughing and trying to outdo his stories. John could have kissed him. Or not. Instead he translated for the benefit of the depleted catering staff, and earned Scott extra helpings of the local dessert: thin pastry folded around honey and nuts, a sticky confection that was the local version of baklava.

The growl of engines cut through the hilarity and inside the tent the silence fell like a lead blanket. Sergeant Morovski appeared in the doorway and stopped, the focus of more than twenty pairs of eyes. John and Mike approached him, Babcock hurrying to join them.

"Is there a problem, Sergeant?" John asked, hearing the journalist translating quietly for Mike's benefit.

"No. I'm here to tell you the insurgents have been scattered, driven away. We'll move you out as soon as possible tomorrow morning. A group of UN soldiers will be here to assist you and my men will guard the convoy." Sighs of relief susurrated through the crowd when Babcock passed it along. "We'll get you all safely to Khorog and onto a charter flight to Dushanbe." He turned on his heel and disappeared into the night before John could relay any of the questions called to him.

"I don't know whether to be relieved or disappointed," Mike said. "Damn it, I hope we can come back to the site—maybe next year. How about you, John? If we manage to get the dig kick-started some time in the future, would you be aboard?"

"Like a shot. Just get in touch with Maria Jaeger at the Bickerstall Agency and she'll see to the arrangements." He'd make sure of it as well, even if he had to call it a vacation as far as MI6 was concerned.

The mess tent emptied quickly. John and Mike lingered long enough to talk with the caterers and make sure they would be there to provide a breakfast first thing in the morning then returned to their tents.

When John walked in and zipped the door shut, Scott was standing by the desk. For a moment he looked uncharacteristically awkward and unsure of himself. Then his cocky grin appeared and he sauntered toward John.

"So it's our last night together," he said. "Want to go out in a blaze of glorious fucking?"

John rolled his eyes. "Your command of the English language never ceases to amaze me. I fully understand why you merely carry a camera; your vocabulary is below the standards of even the tabloid press."

"You're channeling your inner Snape again," Scott said dolefully, taking another step nearer.

"Who?"

"Never mind. Fuck Snape. Why don't you fuck me instead? Or we can switch," he added, hope in his voice. John couldn't stop his chuckle and Scott closed in on him with a sudden pounce.

"I don't think so," he said. "Why don't you take your pallet into the other compartment and I'll be there in a moment. I need to make sure all the excavation reports are packed."

"Okay." But Scott was back as soon as he'd dropped the pallet on the floor, and leaned over John's shoulder as he sat at the desk and booted the laptop.

John skimmed through his excavation

notes, made sure they were all finalized, and signed off on the incomplete reports. Once all the paperwork and the computers were back at Dushanbe University, it would be down to the Archaeology Department there to tidy everything. Then, very aware of Scott's warm breath ghosting over his cheek, he sent an email to the Bickerstall Agency, informing Maria the dig was closing down ahead of schedule and he would be available for more work in a few days—all open and above board, just as any contracted archaeologist would. He logged out, turned off the laptop, and stowed it away in the large case, then finally packed the paper notes, photos, plans, and sketches in there as well. Regret settled in the back of his mind. Not for the covert mission still hanging in the balance, but for his covering role. He'd enjoyed being Doctor John Jones, Assistant Site Director.

"You don't look so happy," Scott said

quietly, slipping his arms around John's shoulders.

"I don't often get the chance at temporary work on an excavation. It's good, being an archaeologist again." He reached up and held Scott's hands over his breastbone. "Then there was the bonus."

"Me."

John laughed. "Maybe," he acknowledged. "You did well in the mess this evening, helping to ease the tension and keep the mood light. Thank you."

"No problem." He nibbled delicately at John's ear. "Do I get a reward?"

"I can probably think of something."

"Thought you might."

John switched off the light and turned his head to capture Scott's mouth. The kiss was awkward, but satisfying. "Let's go to bed," he said.

Game On, Game Over Chris Quinton

# CHAPTER NINE

The UN arrived in the early morning, blue-helmeted soldiers in five armored personnel carriers and a couple of armored patrol vehicles escorting the caterers from Khorog.

"Damn," Scott said quietly, standing in the tent's doorway to watch the convoy's arrival. Then he turned to glance into the tent at John. "Okay, Doc, what can I say? It's been great." His smile was as wide and jaunty as usual, but it didn't quite reach his eyes. "Wish I could say 'see you around', but, hey." He shrugged. "So, uh, goodbye." Then he grabbed his duffel and backpack and strode out of John's life without looking back.

"Goodbye," John murmured, ignoring the twist of pain in his heart. He began to gather up his own and the University's baggage. He'd

*188*

known the score right from the start: just a casual fuck, no strings, and he'd chosen to ignore the simple rule. He pushed the pain and sense of loss deep and locked it away. Time to move on.

All of the archaeologists' equipment, personal luggage, as well as the University's computers and the carefully packed finds, were loaded into one of the carriers with an overflow into another. By then breakfast was ready for everyone, military and civilian. Even Sergeant Morovski and a handful of his men joined them. The UN contingent included six British and six French soldiers, under the command of an American lieutenant, and half of them seemed to speak Russian to some degree. Two of the Brits attached themselves to John, ostensibly bringing him up to date on the latest Premier League soccer dramas. But the pair of supremely self-contained and confident men weren't with the

UN regardless of their blue helmets. They were there to make sure one of MI6's frontline negotiators got out safely.

The atmosphere was surprisingly congenial, despite some despondency among the students. The only discordant note came from Babcock. He was facing up to Lieutenant Andwele, a tall, wide shouldered African-American who appeared to have the patience of a saint.

"I'm not leaving my car here!" Babcock yelled. "It's a rental, for fuck's sake! It'll get totaled if it stays behind and I'll get hammered by the company!"

"Sorry, sir." Andwele was imperturbable. "I can't allow that. You'll travel in the carriers with everyone else."

"The hell I will!"

In John's opinion, the journalist was probably looking to do a U-turn as soon as the escort left them at Khorog. But the car wasn't the only thing to be left behind. The tents and site hut were also staying, though it was unlikely any of them would still be there by nightfall. Catching Daryush's and Azad's gazes, John went over to them to ostensibly shake hands in farewell.

"Thanks, as always," he said quietly. "No fault of yours the wheel came off this one."

"Or yours," Daryush answered. "Watch your back, John, it's a long way to Khorog."

"I know. Listen, grab Babcock's bloody car if you can, before anyone else does. And keep your heads down until all this blows over. Only contact us when the dust settles and it's clear who's come out on top. No sense in risking your necks before then." They nodded solemnly then broke protocol by pulling John into a rib-threatening double embrace.

"Good hunting, James Bond." Daryush

grinned and pounded his back.

"Stay safe," Azad said. "Come back when you can. There's always a place at our hearth for you."

"Now go." Daryush pushed him away. "Before the young American lion decides we're kidnapping you and charges to the rescue." John smiled and shook his head, turning away before the color heating his face betrayed him.


For some time Babcock shouted and blustered before yielding to the inevitable, time in which Mike, with John translating, did the rounds of farewells and sincere thank-yous to the Tajik support staff. Scott hovered restlessly at Babcock's side, but his gaze always drifted back to John.

Loading of the passengers went quickly after that. The students, the carefully packaged finds, Babcock, and Scott were stowed in the first three APCs, leaving the fourth for the lecturers to share with the personal luggage. Mike gazed wistfully over the site before the armored door clanged shut.

Inside, the APC was stuffy, loud, and claustrophobic. The suitcases and duffels were stacked at the front of the vehicle, not leaving much room for the five people crammed together at the back. Anahita and Rosie seemed stoically resigned. Yves wasn't so restrained. His scowl of displeasure rivaled Babcock's and John could only be thankful the journalist was in another carrier.

For a long time no one spoke. The APC jolted over the rough road, steadily taking them farther away from the site and Ishkoshim.

"Will we come back?" Anahita asked suddenly.

"I hope so," Mike said. "I certainly intend to try to arrange it for next year or the year after. Of course, a lot will depend on the political situation. But if this was only a local skirmish it should have died down by then."

"Feuds tend to last a long time," Anahita said with a sigh. "We can only hope—"

The dull thump of a nearby explosion cut into her words.

"Mortar," John said. "Get down on the floor, all of you!" No one argued. They had only just flattened themselves to the metal when another blast filled the APC with ear-crushing sound and choking smoke. A direct hit to the front of the vehicle sent the explosion ripping through with devastating force, tearing open the roof as if a can opener sliced it and flipping the APC onto its side. They were thrown out in a tangled sprawl of limbs, bloodied and battered, but still alive. The luggage packed at the front of the APC took the brunt of the blast, protecting them. The soldier driving it hadn't been so lucky. Blood and torn flesh were spread over the jagged wreck of the vehicle.

John's head rang, his ears were bleeding, but other than that, as far as he could tell he was unhurt. He couldn't hear much, deafened by the concussion of the explosion, and all he could smell was blood and cordite. Muffled sounds which might be a fusillade of returning fire from the Tajik military filtered through his shocked ears; voices were shouting, hands were tugging at him.

"Come on, sir," said a quiet, calm voice. One of his Special Forces escort. "There's a sniper up there as well. We need to get you—" He stopped and rocked forward as a shot struck him in the back, to be absorbed by his bullet-proof vest. Over his shoulder John could see the Tajik soldiers storming up the hillside, dodging among the boulders. "Come on."

John got his legs under him, looked

around and saw the others on their feet as well, and started to make for the nearest APC. Its door was open and Scott filled the opening, waiting to help him inside. Then a club hit him on the thigh and John went down hard.

He must have blacked out for a few moments. He was cold. Pain washed through him in waves, driven by the thundering beat of his heart and the rush of every inhale and exhale. Dust and smoke clogged his throat, his nostrils, and his eyes. Minor discomforts compared to the agony clawing at him, savaging his leg from hip to foot.

"John?" He could just make out the barely audible words, but he was sure the voice was familiar. He tried to put a name to it but couldn't. Hands touched his face, gently, so very gently. "Don't move. There's a tourniquet on your leg. There's a chopper coming in for you, should be here in five, ten at the m—"

"Sir, you have to leave," said another voice, brisk and businesslike and Yorkshire-English. "Go with Mr Babcock."

"No, I—"

"Can't stay, sir. We need to get the convoy moving. Doctor Jones and the other wounded will be medi-vacced out of here very soon."

"Fuck's sake, Scotty!" John recognized that voice as well. "Get your ass over here! The guy knows what he's doing!"

Scott. Yes. Blond hair and sleek muscles, heat and sex and deep, deep pleasure…

"I gotta go." A broken whisper into his hair. "Get better. Don't you dare die! I'll come and see you in the hospital—"

"Scott! Fuck you, *move it!*"

John thought he heard someone shouting, but it sounded far away. The pain was distancing itself as well. Everything was drifting and he thought perhaps he should try to stop it, hold onto something, but Scott wasn't there anymore. And there was no pain in the darkness…

Knowing in his head there are close to twelve pints of blood in the human body was one thing. Seeing so much dripping from jagged metal, soaking into the dirt, and the mangled flesh and bone which recently housed it, was another. And John—masked with gore, more blood pouring from his shattered thigh, splinters of bone protruding—

Scott forced the images to the back of his mind, along with the shockingly raw sense of impending loss. There was nothing he could do for John except look out for John's friends. In the smothering, close quarters of the overcrowded APC, Anahita wept in his arms and he tried to soothe her to the best of his ability. Neither Rosie, Mike, nor Yves was in there with them, and he hoped against hope they'd squeezed into the other APCs. The interior of the carrier was too noisy for him to hear the chopper coming to evacuate the wounded, no matter how he strained his ears. But determination became rock-solid in his core. He would find John Jones again if it was the last thing he did.

At Khorog they, their boxes, and surviving luggage were hustled onto a charter plane, and for the first time Scott was able to do a headcount. The only ones missing were John, Mike, and Yves. He hadn't seen if Mike and Yves were injured; John had been the sole focus of his attention. How long did it take for a man to bleed to death from that kind of wound? Minutes? Less than an hour, for certain. *Oh, God...*

"Ladies,       gentlemen."      Lieutenant Andwele's deep tone cut through the babble of exhausted, emotional voices. "I have a brief update for you to set your minds at rest. You'll be on your way to Dushanbe very soon, and your various embassies will be on hand to give any help you need. The wounded have already been shipped out and they'll be arriving at the hospital in Dushanbe in about ten minutes."

"How many died?" Babcock called, a question no one else seemed ready to ask.

"Four," Andwele replied into the silence, "and eight with injuries ranging from severe to minor, soldiers and civilians. I can't give you any names as yet, but you can make inquiries about the wounded at the hospital. You're all safe now, so have a good flight." He ducked out of the door and the flight attendant closed it behind him.

"Well, shit," Babcock said. "Scotty, tell

me you still got your camera and you took plenty of action shots."

"Yes," he growled. "I got your fucking pictures!" All through the action it was as if his mind had switched to autopilot and he'd damn near filled the memory card. The only time he'd stopped, he'd been at John's side.

"Good." There was a long silence. Babcock didn't speak again until the plane was starting its takeoff run. Then, "He'll be okay," he muttered from the corner of his mouth.

"What?"

"Doc Jones. Femoral artery blood is bright red and it spurts with every heartbeat. His was dark and it was a steady bleed or he'd have been dead in minutes. He's got a fighting chance. Trust me on that, I wasn't born yesterday. And those two guys shadowing him today? They're no more UN than I am." He tapped the side of his nose and winked. "There's a lot more to our Doc than meets the eye. The security services take care of their spooks, Scotty. Just sayin'."

Scott didn't have to bully his way into Dushanbe's hospital to find out about the missing archaeologists. They were all ferried there for checkups, and for the non-nationals, the various embassies sent representatives. Mike, Scott discovered, suffered a broken arm, and Yves a bullet through his left lung. But John wasn't there. Nor was his name on any admissions list. When Scott managed to corner the British Consulate official, he finally got the news he was dreading. The dead had been taken out of the country to the nearest UN base, but the woman would not give him names; the next of kin had yet to be informed.

"Let it go, Scotty," Babcock advised. "There's nothing more you can do. Besides, you're still contracted to me and I got a deadline. I want all the Silk Road shots, and the ones of the attack." Which reminded Scott of a deadline of his own and another job waiting for him now that this one was effectively over.

His baggage had been stowed in the undamaged APC, so it and the laptop wrapped in two pairs of dirty jeans were safe. He copied all the photos he'd taken on the trip—except the ones of John and the long shots where he was easily recognizable—onto CDs and handed them over to Babcock. He wasn't prepared to share John and his loss yet, if ever. Then he booked a seat on the earliest flight out of Dushanbe he could find and sent Jodi Guildenstern an email to let her know he was on his way to London for their meeting.

John had said he lived in London…

Doctor John Jones was gone, and Scott was left with an unexpectedly huge hole in his life. All he retained were some photographs, his memories of the man who triggered every erogenous zone he possessed and drove him higher than he had flown before—and the nebulous image of a bleak hut on a Tajik hillside and the lean Tajik who wore *Hugo Element* cologne.

Thirty-six hours later, Scott kept his date with Jodi, meeting her in the Departures Concourse at Heathrow's Terminal Five. He was over an hour late, too aware he was wan, drawn, and hollow-eyed from lack of sleep, and didn't appreciate her greeting of, "Shit, Scott, you look like road-kill!"

"Yeah, well, it's been a rough week," he muttered as he hugged her. "It's good to see you again, Jo."

"You, too," she answered, but her concern didn't fade. "Are you okay? Really?"

"Yes," he said. "I just—a friend got killed."

"Oh, honey, I'm sorry."

"Yeah. So am I. Listen, I'm going to grab something from the bookstore. Want anything?"

"No, I'm good. Don't be long, Scott. They'll be calling our flight soon."

"'Kay." He hurried into the store, chose a couple of bags of assorted candies, picked up the latest Harlan Coben paperback, and headed for the checkout. His route took him past the magazine racks, and there he paused.

The image on the front of the glossy magazine was of Cesare Borgia, the striking face with its narrow mouth and deep-set eyes catching Scott's attention. The banner below held it:

*"Human nature has changed very little in the millennia we've walked upright," says*

*Aidan Whittaker, translator of the new-found Borgia letters. "The only differences now are our enhanced abilities to create and destroy."*

He stared at the words, his gut clenching as if expecting a punch. His surroundings faded away and the commotion in the busy store became a muted buzzing in his ears, unable to drown out the crystal clear memory of John's rich voice proclaiming his heartfelt conviction. They'd been alone on that hillside above the dig. No one could have overheard those words, spoken so eloquently straight from John's heart. Moving like an automaton, Scott took the magazine—*History & Archaeology*—from the rack. Aidan Whittaker? Who the fuck was he? How had he gotten hold of John's line and why was he stealing it?

"Scott!" Jodi called from outside the store. "Come on! Our flight's boarding in five!"

He didn't stop to think, just added the

magazine to his paperback and the candy, and headed for the checkout. He'd read the article on the flight to Africa.

PART TWO - GAME OVER

## CHAPTER ONE

If Scott thought Tajikistan was his baptism by fire, four months in Darfur taught him differently. Before they went on to Somalia, he and Jodi spent a month in Cape Town while he recovered from malaria and restored his physical and emotional strength. He also assessed the magazine article. He'd read Aidan Whittaker's piece so many times he could quote the whole thing, word for word, and became convinced there was a lot more to this than met the eye. Every sentence spoke to him of John. He could close his eyes and *hear* John's voice delivering them. Commonsense told him John could have written the article under another name weeks—months—before he died, but the what-ifs haunted Scott.

Brisk, no-nonsense Jodi spent that month with him, the older sister he didn't have, and for the first time he talked about the Silk Road job, the dig, John. Because he was half out of his head with a 103 degree fever, he maybe said more than he intended. Jodi didn't comment, didn't pressure him, at first. She waited until he was back to his usual jaunty health and they were putting together the final preparations for their next mission in Somalia.

"You have to find out exactly what happened to John," Jodi said out of the blue. "And what the link is between him and Whittaker. Or you'll never find real closure."

"Shit, Jodi, I don't need closure! The guy was someone I knew for a few days. We spent two nights fucking, he got shot and died. End of story." But he knew it wasn't. Just saying it brought back those nights, and the nightmare on the road to Khorog: John bleeding to death and Scott leaving him, simply climbing into the APC and letting himself be driven away. For one sickening moment he could smell the blood, the cordite, the dust.

Jodi wasn't taking any notice. "I can help you," she continued. "I've got all kinds of contacts in weird places. When we're done with Somalia, I'll see what I can shake out of the tree."

"No, leave it," Scott muttered. "It isn't going to change anything."

"Okay." Jodi held up her hands in surrender. "Have it your way, but you're wrong."

Darfur had been tough, far more so than Scott had expected, despite Jodi's warnings. Somalia turned out to be worse. Their planned two months became four, two weeks of which were spent on the run from a contingent of pirates and hiding out in a remote village. Then Scott and his cameras were hired to accompany a journalist on an expedition in Tibet for two months, and another month in Nepal. He finally returned to America and crashed with friends in Florida, and slept for twenty-four hours. For a couple of weeks he chilled out on the beach, resettling himself in a lifestyle that at first seemed utterly surreal after the last year. He hooked up a few times, until he realized he was choosing older men with dark hair, brown eyes, and lean bodies, so he simply got drunk instead.

Jodi's email came out of the blue, and he read it squint-eyed and hung over. It took two more reads before he got the gist of it.

*Hi, Scott,*

*I know you won't have Googled your archaeologist or the mystery man, so I did. No website, no social network for either of them, but the* History & Archaeology *magazine has regularly published articles by JJ over the last twelve, thirteen years but nothing for at least a year. Over the same time scale, AW doesn't show up anything like as often, but he is out there. Since the Borgia article, they've published one by him in the last seven months, and the latest has only just come out*—The Magyar and the Rom, Past and Present. *AW's also a regular, if infrequent, contributor to* Ancient Voices, *and the editor there is a friend of a friend of my agent. Get in touch with Gerald Dobson, edgd@ancientwords.com. Maybe he can tell you something about AW. Keep in touch, Scott. I want to know how all this pans out \*g\*.*

    *Take care of yourself.*

    *Jodi*

    Scott deleted the email. Then hauled it out of the trash folder and left it in the inbox. He vacillated for a week then did some research on the magazine itself. The publisher, In Academia Press, had its head office in Oxford, and *Ancient Voices* was one of half a dozen titles in its stable. Scott stared at the laptop screen, not seeing it. His gaze focused inward, to images of John Jones and the heat in his eyes, the sensuality of his mouth—when it wasn't thinned in irritation or stubbornness. Scott started to chuckle quietly until the pain of the memories stopped it in his throat. He missed the man. But John was dead. Wasn't he?

The similarities of word usage couldn't be just a coincidence, couldn't be clutching at straws. If there was only the flimsiest of chances John might still be alive, he needed to know for sure. Scott booked the first flight he could find to London.

* * * *

Oxford was a hotbed of cars and bicycles vying for dominance on the narrow streets. Ancient and modern buildings stood shoulder to shoulder, with occasional glimpses of tranquil quadrangles through the colleges' medieval archways. The impression Scott got was of a town at ease with itself, firmly rooted in its past and reaching toward the future.

The offices of In Academia Press were on the third floor above a range of shops. He hadn't made an appointment to see the editor, working on the theory that a highbrow, high-priced monthly magazine wouldn't be busy behind the scenes. He was wrong. A harassed middle-aged woman was stuffing folded paper into envelopes, sealing them and tossing them into an out tray already close to overflowing. His request to see Mr Dobson was turned down flatly if politely.

"It's really important," he persisted, using his eyes and smile to the full. She didn't even blink.

"Impossible," she said curtly. "His

earliest free time is at ten o'clock on Wednesday of next week. That's the best I can offer you."

"Then maybe you could help?" he suggested winningly. "Aidan Whittaker—he's a friend of a friend of mine, and I have some urgent news to pass on. Can you give me any idea where I can find him?"

"Absolutely not. Contributor confidentiality is one of our watchwords, young man."

"Okay, good, so if I give you a note from me, would you send it to him?" For a second, she wavered. "Please? It really is important. His pal, John Jones—he's an archaeologist—he—"

"Very well," she interrupted, "but you'll need to be quick."

"Thank you! Uh, can I borrow a pen? And a piece of paper?"

The frown she gave him should have scorched, but he bore up bravely. She handed over pen and paper, and he scribbled quickly. *Hi, Aidan, I'm in London. Call me ASAP, Scott.* He scrawled his cell phone number at the bottom and handed pen and paper back. While he'd been writing, he'd watched her from the corner of his eye, hoping her instruction to be quick meant what he hoped. She sorted through the envelopes and sheets awaiting her attention, and put one of each aside. Then she took his note from him, folded it with her own paper, and slid both into the envelope, then dropped it on top of the pile. He glanced over, read the upside-down address, and thanked her profusely.

Scott found a chain motel on the edge of Oxford and waited. No phone call came and by the time two weeks were up, Scott's initial euphoria was gone. John-Aidan had either not received the letter or, more likely, saw no reason to call him back. Not even for old times' sake. Which was fair enough. Their parting had been casual to the point of brusqueness. But that was before the insurgents' attack and the mortar strike, though Scott didn't know why it should make a difference.

Taking out his notepad, he opened it to the page where he'd written Aidan's address: 1 Cove Cottages, Green Street, Avebury, Wiltshire. Then he Googled the place. He found a tiny village of barely three hundred souls, clustered in and around a huge ring of stones which predated it by thousands of years.

"I'm not a stalker," he said aloud. "I just want to make sure it's him and he's alive. Not even gonna say hi."

He left the next morning.

Two and a half hours later, Scott pulled into the parking lot on the outskirts of Avebury.

It was raining, which gave him a good reason to be wearing a ball cap with the hood of his waterproof jacket over it, rendering him unrecognizable. He hoped. Just in case John-Aidan was crazy enough to be wandering around in the rain.

Water dripped from the bill of Scott's cap as he headed slowly down Green Street. His goal was off to his left, a pair of picturesque, semidetached thatched cottages hunched against the weather. Lights showed in their windows, comforting glows in the gloom of the day. Scott imagined a blazing log fire, John sprawling in a large armchair, a glass of beer in his hand... and himself sitting on the carpet, leaning back against John's legs, John's hand moving gently though his hair... Scott shook himself and turned back, crossing to the far side of the road.

He'd taken only a few steps when he heard a door shut behind him. A gate squeaked and clanged, and fast, uneven footsteps came toward him. Keeping his head down, Scott looked sideways.

It was John, no question, though he was bundled up in a raincoat. He wore no hat, and his unmistakable profile could be easily seen. The surge of relief and joy hit Scott like an emotional battering ram. He almost called out John's name, had taken a single step off the pavement, before he caught himself back. John-Aidan hadn't phoned him. This was a new name, a new life, one where Scott Landon didn't have a place.

Yet Scott saw more than he was comfortable with. Rain poured down John's face, plastering his dark hair to his skull and dripping from the end of his nose. He walked with the aid of a cane, his shoulders bowed a little, his body listing slightly to one side as if he relied on the cane for support and balance. His face was pale and more gaunt than Scott remembered. John looked and moved like a man old before his time.

Scott's heart twisted and his breath caught in his lungs, and once more he nearly called John's name. But he swallowed it down, just stood there in the rain, and watched Aidan Whittaker limp across the road and disappear into the Red Lion pub.

*Okay, puzzle solved*, he told himself. *Curiosity satisfied.* Babcock had guessed right; John Jones had probably been a spook, and now he was back to being a historian while he waited for the next assignment. Unless the damaged leg meant he was permanently off the active list. Scott knew he should go now. But he couldn't. Not yet. Slowly he followed in Aidan's wake but didn't enter the pub. Instead he peered through one of the windows. Aidan was just visible, sitting alone in a corner with one leg stretched out and his cane propped against the side of his chair. He was nursing a cup of something—tea or coffee—and his expression was introspective and sad. The phantom pain lodged under Scott's ribs. He turned away quickly and hurried back to his car. He did not dare stay longer, or he'd be in the pub receiving the patented Doctor Jones's Ice-Cold Stare, to which only Brent Babcock proved immune. But every instinct told him to just push open the door, walk into the bar, and say, "Hi, I've missed you."

Scott intended to go back to London, but instead drove the few miles to Marlborough and booked into a room at the first hotel he saw. For a long time he sat on the bed and tried to process his feelings. He needed to talk to someone, but the only one who knew about his connection with John was Jodi, and she was in Geneva, the last he'd heard. So he emailed her instead.

*JJ's alive and he's AW.*

The answer came back almost immediately. *So what are you doing about it? What does he say?*

*I'm not doing anything.*

*Did you actually speak to the man? No, of course you didn't. Scott, this is me giving you a virtual slap upside the head. Talk to him!*

He logged out of the laptop and closed it without answering. When his cell phone rang a few minutes later, he wasn't surprised to see Jodi's name on the small screen.

No greeting, no preliminaries, just Jodi's impatient, "Talk to him!"

"I can't. There's nothing to say."

"Bullshit!"

"It's true, Jodi. It was just a couple of nights fucking. Didn't mean anything to either of us."

"So why are you eating your heart out right now?"

"I—" He stopped and the silence stretched.

"Damn it!" Jodi snapped. "Listen, you dumb jerk, maybe it started out that way, but obviously there was the potential for more between you, or you wouldn't be in this mess, right? Of course, right! So you do something about it!"

"How can I? Do what?"

"God, I should be a *yenta*! You start over, of course! You go the 'Hi, I'm Scott, nice to meet you' route. You get to know each other, find out if you can be friends before you're fuck-buddies this time. See where it takes you."

"He doesn't want to know!"

"You don't know that! And stop whining. What are you, twelve?"

"I sent him my number two weeks ago.

He didn't call me."

"Why would he? Probably thought all you wanted was a fast fuck to pass the time. Be his friend, for God's sake, before you jump his bones."

"Okay! I'll think about it." He paused and sighed ruefully. "Thanks, Jodi."

"Do more than think!" she advised. "I gotta go—update me!"

"Yeah," he said, but she'd already ended the call.

Scott stared at the wall, eyes unfocussed. Start over. Yes, he could do that. But first there would have to be some careful planning. It would probably take a month or two, but he could cope.

It took a little more than a month for Scott to find his way into the Avebury community. Marlborough's Tourist Information office provided him with a list of names and phone numbers of people in the area who did vacation lets. All of them were booked up throughout the year, but he left his cell number with them just in case…

Then Mrs Hamilton, who ran a small B&B at 4 Green Street, called him back. Someone near her lived in a rented, furnished cottage but was planning to move away from the village in the next month or so. Was he still interested? The address was 2 Cove Cottages. Scott welcomed it as a good omen.

Now all he needed to do was find a legitimate reason to be in Avebury in the first place.

# CHAPTER TWO

Aidan opened the front door and stepped out, carefully blocking the ginger and white cat who lived down the road and preventing it from sneaking past him into the cottage. The maneuver nearly cost him his balance, but his heavy cane was firmly planted and his dignity remained intact. Yesterday the cat won through, and it had taken half an hour of cajoling and a quantity of cold chicken, which should have been his lunch, before the bloody thing permitted itself to be lured out. Yet another battle in the war begun months ago, the day he moved into the cottage.

A much more pleasant acquaintance was his next door neighbor, Maggie Trimm, and her infant daughter. Both were pretty, laughing people with brown hair, rosebud mouths, and dimples. Maggie always had a smile and a cheerful hello for him. Today was no different, even though a rental van was parked outside her cottage, and she was running back and forth carrying the last few carefully wrapped breakables. He paused long enough to wish her good luck in her new home and new job; then, taking a deep, refreshing lungful of the clean, honeysuckle- and lavender-scented air, Aidan set off along Green Street toward the pub.

Some days were better than others, and when the stiffness and pain in his rebuilt thigh were particularly bad, like today, the walking stick became a necessity. Aidan hated it, but accepted it as a temporary evil. His damaged muscles were strengthening all the time. He'd probably always have a slight limp, but he could live with that. At least his leg was still 99% his own, and no thanks to the sniper's bullet.

He'd been in the village six months now and the locals were beginning to get used to him. It helped that he dressed conventionally if casually, had neatish, shortish, dark hair silvering at the temples, and did not blither nonsense about ley lines, crop circles, solstices, and druidic celebrations. Most of Avebury's long-term inhabitants were heartily fed up with those over the years, and did not relish the prospect of another resident loony.

There'd been some qualms voiced when he disclosed he was a writer, but those were quickly dispelled. He wrote articles for highbrow journals on esoteric stuff such as *The Development of Modern Languages*, or *The Roots of Russian*, and *The Magyar and the Rom, Past and Present*.

Safe. That was Aidan Whittaker.

Safe. That was how Aidan felt as he waited on the corner for a bus to pass then hobbled quickly across the main road. Safe in a small community that on one level was so quintessentially English it ought to be preserved under a dome in perpetuity. It had only one drawback: the largest circle of standing stones yet discovered, a circle of prehistoric, sacred space wide enough to encompass a good part of the village, elevating it to Tourist Magnet status. A definite bonus was the post office with its small but useful general store, and the Red Lion public house, both within easy walking distance of the cottage.

All potential inconveniences were far outweighed by one simple fact: Avebury was as far as it was possible to get from the potential tinderboxes of the world and still be on the same planet. Aidan did not miss the adrenaline-pumping danger of his previous career at all. Well, not often. And if he occasionally—often—thought about an archaeological site in Tajikistan and a certain blond American, those memories were swiftly slammed down and locked away.

His new home, 1 Cove Cottages and its attached, not-quite-mirror-twin were both owned by Omega Investments, a long-standing London-based company, and the six hundred year old cottage had been thoroughly renovated and furnished prior to his arrival.

The previous occupant had lived there for close to seventy years, and until his death used every legal method possible to prevent Omega doing much more than essential maintenance. By the time Aidan moved in, the cottage had a reconnected telephone, and sported a newly thatched roof, secondary double-glazing on the windows, as well as central heating, and broadband internet connection. All modern conveniences in a one bedroom cottage on the edge of a village set in a wide, shallow valley.

The pub was a godsend. Aidan enjoyed

its beer, food, and ambiance, and was doing his subtle best to be taken under the locals' communal cloak. It did not hurt that he was both knowledgeable and enthusiastic about cricket, as he'd quietly told the barman, Tom, a week or so after his arrival. It was only the dodgy leg keeping him from asking about joining the local cricket club. He used to be a damned good seam bowler before the car crash.

Well, the vehicle *had* crashed. The inhabitants of Avebury didn't need to know a direct hit from a Taliban-supplied mortar shell had been responsible. Tom had sympathized and introduced him to some fellow cricket enthusiasts, and now Aidan was well on the way to acceptance by the pub's regulars and the wider village. After all, he intended to live there for quite a while. Years, if he was lucky.

Being signed off as medically unfit for active duty meant he had the choice of a fresh start, or permanent desk duty at MI6 HQ. Aidan chose the former. He would finally be able to take back his real name and work full-time at his first love—linguistics and translator of obscure texts, ancient and comparatively modern. But he occasionally missed the gut-wrenching adrenaline surge of danger and run-for-your-life, once an integral part of John Jones's career as a negotiator between hostiles.

The twinges of pain in his leg reminded him Jones didn't exist anymore. Aidan Whittaker survived to be closing in on his fortieth birthday and now lived a good, if quiet, existence. But John Jones left other memories behind him: a fair-haired American with a cocky grin and a charmingly mischievous glitter in his blue eyes, his lean, tanned body writhing and arching under John's hands and mouth. A man with a quick intelligence and an outgoing personality, vibrant with life. A potent combination, and a tenacious one.

For a very short while Scott had needed more than casual sex, though he probably hadn't known it. So when the time came for them to part, it was just a laid-back, "It's been great." And, "So, uh, goodbye."

Scott Landon had slid right past John's defenses, and now lodged deep in Aidan's heart despite all efforts to evict him. Which was all the reason Aidan needed to ignore the request tucked in with his royalties statement from *Ancient Voices*. He neither knew nor cared why Charlotte agreed to add the note to his envelope; more importantly, she'd assured him over the phone she hadn't passed on his address. Fast fucks with men fourteen years his junior were not on Aidan's agenda. Landon could find someone else to scratch his itch. But the memories had awoken, and they hurt. So did the loneliness. He had his academic life back, but the emptiness he'd suddenly discovered within himself was unexpected and unwelcome.

* * * *

Aidan made his cautious way into the pub. The cheerful, undemanding company of Tom and the regulars would go a long way toward improving his mood, and a round of the home-cured, thick-sliced ham sandwiches, courtesy of Ellie-in-the-kitchen, suited his needs. Especially with a pint of Badger Champion ale.

The place seemed unusually busy, given it was midday in the middle of the week in late spring. The increased clientele didn't have the look of coach passengers brought in to 'do' the circle of stones and the village. Aidan hesitated on the threshold of the saloon, and behind the bar, Tom greeted him with a smile and a nod.

"The usual?" he asked, already reaching for a glass.

Aidan shook off his wariness. "Yes, please, and ham sandwiches to go with it, plus whatever you're drinking." He perched on a barstool and leaned closer. "What's the occasion?"

"Thanks," Tom said. "I'll have a mineral water. It's another film crew," he went on with a snicker of amused derision. "Doing 'Specters of Old England'."

"You're kidding me."

"Nope. The Walkers are already concocting a few new tales to pass along. After all, the ghosts of Florrie and the Barber-Surgeon have been done to death in more ways than one." The names ran together, though Aidan guessed there must have been four hundred years or more between the two fatalities.

"Florrie and the Barber-Surgeon." Aidan

tuned out the old men's voices and turned back to the bar, grinning. "They sound like a music hall act."

"They do, at that." Tom chuckled and placed a pint of dark nectar in front of him. "I'm damn sure the Walkers have bored you silly about them, and if they haven't, Ellie has. 'Our Florrie has a fancy for dark-haired men'," he falsettoed in a fair imitation of the pub's heading-toward-elderly cook.

"Now you come to mention it," Aidan smiled. "Though I haven't actually felt any spectral fingers running through my hair so far. No one really believes this barber-surgeon haunts the stones, surely?"

Tom tapped the side of his nose. "There's some who've heard his screams," he said solemnly.

"By the name of Walker?" They shared a grin and raised a toast to local imagination and enterprise; the Brothers Walker garnered themselves plenty of free drinks on the strength of the supposed hauntings. "How come the barber-surgeon isn't in the local museum?" Aidan queried. "I meant to ask weeks ago, but I had deadlines to meet and it kept slipping my mind."

"Because he got blown to smithereens."

Aidan raised his eyebrows in surprise. "Oh? What happened?"

"Hitler happened. His bones were sent to London for some reason, and during the war the museum took a direct hit."

"Poor sod was doomed from beginning to end," Aidan observed and raised his glass again. "To retribution."

"Amen," said Tom and drank as well.

After a few more minutes of desultory conversation, Aidan retired to his usual corner table and to all intents and purposes, sank into a reverie.

* * * *

Ellie-in-the-kitchen brought his sandwiches over and plunked them down on the battered but clean table. She'd been generous with the ham and side salad, and he gave her the gently affectionate smile which made him one of her favorites.

"Thank you," he said. "You're a star, Ellie."

"Huh," she said. "Got to do something to feed you up. Sure you don't want soup with it? It's cucumber and watercress today."

"No, thanks. This is fine. How long is the film crew staying?"

"Not long, I hope." Ellie scowled across the room, her ire focused on the brotherly trio. "All we need now is that pair of benighted idiots from Bennett's caravan field with their druidic nonsense and bed sheets, and old Marge Compton with her ley lines, and the circus will be complete."

"Bed sheets?" Aidan gazed at her, sandwich halfway to his mouth.

"Cobbled together to make white dresses—robes, they insist on calling 'em. Bloody daft, as far as I'm concerned. How's that Maggie Trimm? I hear she's leaving soon."

"Today," he answered. "Most of the time I don't even know she's there, but I'll miss seeing her around." The cottage walls were whitewashed chalk and flint and easily two feet thick, and provided very effective soundproofing.

"Ah." It was a disappointed sound. "I'd heard she got herself a job and a flat in Marlborough."

"Yes. She'll find more opportunities for

her and the baby in a large town." Aidan smiled. Although there hadn't been a problem with his young neighbor, he rather liked the idea of an empty house beside him.

## CHAPTER THREE

Maggie moved out on Tuesday. On Wednesday the Property Management refurbishing team went through the small cottage to either prepare for the next occupant or mothball it.

After two days of frenetic activity, peace descended on Green Street, the film crew departed, and things returned to normal. Solitude. Peace and quiet. His cottage became a haven again, the cat resumed his/her regime of grand larceny with menaces, and the newly opening roses added their scents to the honeysuckle. Aidan picked up the threads of his current article. There was a deadline, after all.

With the article completed and sent, Aidan became aware he was both hungry and thirsty. Emails sat in his inbox and paper letters in his plastic pending tray, but they could wait.

He stood up and stretched the kinks out of his back and shoulders, pressing his palms against the ceiling between the heavy black beams, and then limped into the kitchen at the rear of the cottage. It and the small, ground floor bathroom had been added a mere ninety years ago, but now boasted fully modern appliances and ceilings a good twelve inches higher than the other two rooms. The kitchen door was glazed, and opened into a conservatory, little more than a tacked-on greenhouse. Just big enough for a cane chair and a side table, it still offered a clear path to the all-glass back door proper, giving a clear view of the garden between high hedges of privet and dog roses. For a moment, Aidan paused and contemplated the view.

As well as densely planted herbs and flowerbeds and an irregular-shaped area of lawn, the garden boasted an aged apple tree, a bench seat beneath a wooden pergola smothered in more honeysuckle, and a small potting shed almost completely swamped under the enthusiastic merging of a climbing rose (color as yet unknown) and a blue clematis. It was, like the village, stereotypically English and oddly restful. It would be a pleasant place to work, come the summer—

A car drew up outside and stopped. For no apparent reason, tension jarred across Aidan's nerves and down his spine. His hand closed convulsively over the head of his cane and he turned quickly toward the door. Outside a car door slammed, then silence fell. Aidan was no longer on any kind of list, active or otherwise, but it counted for nothing. All those months away from the department couldn't dull his instincts and reactions.

Aidan moved swiftly to the living room and peered cautiously out of the window. There was a silver BMW parked in front of the neighboring cottage and the garden gate was open. Then his phone rang.

To his credit, Aidan didn't jump. But the adrenaline surge ratcheted his pulse up a few notches. It was probably Gerald, his *Voices* editor, calling to acknowledge the receipt of the article and rip him a new one for leaving it so close to the wire. Even so, he hesitated a long time before lifting the receiver from its rest.

"Hi," said an achingly familiar voice, and Aidan felt as if his heart and lungs had seized. "I'm next door. Care for a drink at the Lion?"

Over a year later, and the lazy drawl, redolent of America's southwestern states, still stopped his breath and raised a shiver down his spine. He shouldn't let it. He couldn't allow the man to get under his armor again. The unwanted obsession he'd developed for Scott, and the need in him for something more meaningful, permanent, left him vulnerable to someone who was surely only interested in casual sex. Not that Scott's lust would be a problem once the man had taken a good look at him. Aidan knew only too well he was a long way from the physical condition he'd been in a year ago. But his blood was already heating, thickening his cock and accelerating his pulse. Self-preservation dictated the most effective defense: attack.

"Scott Landon. What the hell are you doing here?" There was only the one sibilant in the sentences, but Aidan made the most of it.

"Working." Aidan could too easily picture Scott's cocky smile. "You're a hard man to find, John. Oh, sorry. Aidan."

Aidan's stomach clenched painfully. "Yes," he snapped. "That was the idea, so you've got some explaining to do." On the one hand he was both furious and elated the man had sought him out. On the other he was quietly panicked. How the hell did Scott identify him, let alone find him? If a photo-journalist could track him down in his retirement, so could old enemies who might think he still had up-to-date knowledge to spill. The only weapons in the house were sharp kitchen knives. But he was trained in various lethal methods of offensive defense, and didn't necessarily require conventional weapons. "How did you trace me?"

"Uh, that spiel you gave me at the dig? About how we haven't changed as a species, just got better at creating and destroying? It kind of stuck with me. I thought you'd died," Scott continued, the sudden harshness in his voice cutting into Aidan. "Then I saw that magazine cover with your quote on the front and—" He broke off and when he spoke again, his voice was lighter, bordering on flippant. "No one could have overheard you back then, and you've got a distinctive writing style. So I read that article on those Borgia letters, the ones they found in the Santa Veronica nunnery in Tuscany. Even without the quote, there was something about the turn of phrase that said John Jones to me. Only it was written by this Aidan Whittaker guy. So there was him and Doc Jones and Faraz, and I didn't know what to think. Whatever, I owe you a meal at the very least. Faraz saved my life, remember?"

He remembered very well and it was pointless to deny it. He remembered, too, the nights they'd spent in his tent, trying desperately to be silent, once he'd given in to Scott's determined attempts at seduction. It had been a case of mutual lust in the dust, he reminded himself. Just fucking. No reason at all to expect anything more, then and especially now. Nor would there be an action replay, and if Scott had plans along those lines, the randy sod was in for a nasty shock.

Scott, working in Avebury. If there was a god of cosmic coincidences, he, she, or it must be laughing themselves sick. There was only one course of action he could take: keep the bloody man at bay. Or make the attempt, at least.

But part of him wanted to hear the rest of Scott's explanation, catch up with his news. Okay, he could do both. He was an ex-MI6 operative, for God's sake. "You're buying," Aidan said. "And it includes a meal. I'm hungry." He slammed the phone down and stamped out of the front door.

Aidan's dramatic exit was marred by his limp and the cat. It hurtled between his legs in a bi-colored blur, invading the cottage before he could prevent it.

"Damn it!" he yelled. "Now look what

you've done!"

"Me?" Scott's head appeared over the privet hedge. "What did I do?"

"Shut up! What the hell are you really doing here?"

Sky-blue eyes widened in innocent surprise. "I already told you. Living. And working. It's a calendar shoot. Seasons in a Landscape—"

"What?" The man was talking pure gibberish as far as Aidan was concerned.

Scott sighed and rolled his eyes heavenward. "You obviously need a beer. What's your cat's name?"

"Bugger the cat! How—"

"Damned odd name for a cat. Or anything else. What's the poor critter done to you?"

Aidan took a deep, calming breath. "It is not my cat," he said slowly and clearly. "I do not know its name. I don't want to know its name. I want to know why you're here, and," he went on, voice rising, "who the hell told you who I was and how did you get my phone number?"

Scott's smile showed an unwarranted expanse of white teeth. "Definitely a beer. With a whisky chaser. Come on, we can talk over the meal."

"There's nothing to talk about."

"Yes, there is," Scott said, wounded to the quick if those soulful eyes were to be believed. Which Aidan didn't, not for an instant. "Don't tell me you've forgotten Tajikistan! You were working for some university, and I was taking photos for that book on the Silk Road—" As if Aidan was a child and needed it explained in See-Spot-Run simplicity.

"I've retired, damn it!"

"Brent was right! You are a spook!"

Scott sounded as gleeful as a schoolboy meeting David Beckham.

"I was not, damn it!" Aidan snapped. "I was trying to negotiate an intertribal deal and you and Babcock came close to scuppering it!" And he did not want to discuss it. Not the archaeological excavation, or the rescue, or the few nights they'd shared before the dig closed down and everyone was convoyed out by a combined force of Tajik and United Nations troops. Or the mortar shell that struck his APC, or the sniper's shot that wrecked his MI6 career, or any pie-in-the-sky chance of continuing the whatever-it-was John Jones started with Scott Landon. He was Aidan Whittaker these days, just a freelance writer with a rebuilt thighbone that might or might not let him reclaim a more active life in the future.

He swung out of the gate and headed for the pub, ignoring the ache in his heart. The bloody cat would be dealt with later, evicted so forcefully that when it returned from its boot-assisted, impromptu flight into the next county, it would never set paw across his threshold again.

"Hey," said his new neighbor, catching up with him. "How's the leg? It looked pretty bad. Uh, is it a prosthetic? Did they manage to save it? When did you get out of the hospital?"

"Yes, they saved it," Aidan said curtly. "I was released ten months ago."

"Thank God." Scott's voice was warm with sympathy. "I did try to find out what happened to you, but when I couldn't find your name at the hospital and they told me—" He paused while they waited for the road to clear, as if there was more he wanted to say but couldn't find the right words. "Nice cane," he finished lamely.

Aidan glared at Scott, taking in the trim,

tan slacks and fitted white polo shirt which defined long muscles and pointed up the man's suntan. He could recall every detail of every glorious inch of the body beneath those clothes. "Why don't you just bugger off and do your calendar shoot somewhere else? I hear the Orkneys are nice this time of year."

Scott seemed impervious to his hostility. That, too, was painfully familiar. "Nope. Has to be Avebury. The heart of England," he intoned, hand on breast. "Or is it the soul? Whatever."

"Bullshit. How did you know I was here, and how did you get my phone number?" No one at MI6 would have passed on the change of name and personal details, and Charlotte had sworn—

"I found more of Aidan Whittaker's stuff in another 'zine—*Ancient Voices*—so I went to Oxford and visited their office."

"They gave you my details?" Aidan

demanded furiously.

"Uh, not exactly." Scott's grin was boyish and unapologetically pleased. "I might have kinda watched the secretary's out tray when she put the envelope in it. The one with my note inside. I can read upside-down and the name was Whittaker. So I took a chance, Googled Avebury, hunted down the places up for rent, and found out next door was gonna be vacant. It seemed like an omen, so I grabbed it. The phone was easy. The lady across the street had the number from when some old guy lived there."

Aidan stared at him, momentarily speechless and unable to comprehend why the man had gone to so much trouble to track him. "Fine! Just stay out of my way! If I wanted to renew our nonexistent relationship, Mr Landon, I would have phoned you!" Leaving Scott standing, Aidan hobbled across the road in front of a tractor and made for the door of the pub. But Scott got there before him and held it open, a Cheshire cat smile on his face. Aidan snarled wordlessly and stalked to the bar. "Tom, this is Scott Landon, he's just moved into the place next door to me. He photographs things." The tone of his voice suggested unnatural practices.

"Hi, Tom," Scott said, unabashed by the implied slander. "Aidan's usual, Glenlivet for me, and whatever you're having."

"A photographer, Mr Landon?" Tom asked, drawing Aidan's pint.

"Freelance and on commission. Please, call me Scott. I'm going to be here at least a year and I never did like formality."

"Hah!" Aidan snorted and reached past him for the menu.

"You two know each other?" Tom grinned, putting the pint on the bar and picking up a shot glass. He stuck it under the optic then lined it up beside the pint.

"Off and on, while Aidan was working overseas." Scott grinned back, placing money on the bar.

He'd made it sound as if it was more than a few days' acquaintance. "More off than on," Aidan added, before the idiot could launch into some elaborate flight of fancy. "We were in the same place once."

"Here's to journalism and its many facets." Scott lifted his whisky in a salute.

"Well, it's a small world," the barman said cheerfully.

"You can say that again," Aidan muttered in disgust. "Too bloody small. I'll have the salmon starter, the sixteen ounce rump steak done rare with all the trimmings and Ellie's red wine sauce, and her orange and Cointreau sorbet for dessert."

"You're pushing the boat out," Tom

chuckled.

"Yes," Aidan said. "He's paying."

He stumped over to his corner and sat down, stretching out his right leg and massaging his knee. It was aching, but not enough to have him reaching for his pills. Medication outside the strict regimen was a last resort. Over by the bar, Scott was leaning both elbows on the polished wood, chatting companionably with Tom. His blond, slightly too long hair was curling on his collar and over his forehead. Aidan sneered, smothering the gut-deep draw of the man with a false, desperate contempt. What was it, the Windswept Poet look? Or the Rakish-But-Soulful Adventurer? Either way, there was no one in the village who'd be dazzled by it. And what the hell were they talking about? If Scott was regaling the barman with wild and improbable tales, he was certainly a dead man.

It had been so peaceful for the last six months...

## CHAPTER FOUR

The evening went from bad to worse. Ellie-in-the-kitchen brought the starters—Scott ordered the same as him—and the bastard flirted outrageously with her. If Ellie hadn't responded with her usual amused cynicism, Aidan would have taken his fork and stuck it in Scott's neck. Even so, it was clear by the second course the foolish old biddy approved of the interloper.

"At last someone's got you eating a decent-sized meal," she commented as she plunked the platter of steak in front of him. "I hope he keeps it up. It'll do you and our profits good."

"Glad to be of service." Scott beamed at her and leaned across to wink at Aidan. "The food wasn't as good in Tajikistan, was it?"

Aidan stitched a smile on his face. "I remember a horse who thought it was okay. The one who made you suffer. Remember?" It was a threat and a warning, if the cretin was smart enough to cotton on.

"Hell, yes!" Scott laughed. "Ellie, I couldn't sit down for a month. I think I've still got the scars. Want to see?" He stood up and started to undo his belt.

"No, thanks," she said, snickering. "I prefer my rump steaks ready for grilling. You're a bad man, Scott Landon." Which, coming from her, was an accolade.

By the time they'd finished eating, the regulars were beginning to fill up the bar. Inevitably, the Walker brothers homed in on the newcomer and the old frauds took it in turns to hold forth in their well-polished routine. Scott was both fascinated and delighted if his wide grin was anything to go by.

Aidan tried to ignore them, but failed.

"Ah, well, back in the Middle Ages," he overheard from Walter, "the folks around here used to have a go at them stones every now and then. Broke some up and used 'em for building the cottages, hauled some away, planted others."

"They'd dig a pit beside a stone," Fred went on, "heave it over into the hole and bury it. Only sometimes accidents happened, and them stones are bloody big."

"He were what they called a barber-surgeon," Walter continued, "and he'd made enemies. One night he was pushed into the hole and they made the stone fall on him and left him. He were trapped—crushed—and though he screamed somethin' terrible, no one came to dig him out."

Harry took up the tale. "So when they started to excavate between the Wars, under one of them buried stones they found the skeleton of a man. There were scissors and a lancet, and some silver coins among the bones, so they knew who he was, and when they put the stone back upright the way it should be, that's what the stone was called."

"Wow," Scott said reverently. "Guys, that's amazing. Tell me more! Hey, Tom, can we have another round over here?"

Aidan groaned.

The Walkers didn't need much encouragement.

Florence Smith—better known as Florrie—had been the barmaid and wife to George, an ostler at the inn. She'd possessed a wandering eye, according to the Walkers, a pair of round heels, and a pathological inability to say 'no'. George finally snapped when he caught her behind the bar with her skirts around her waist and her legs around a soldier. Later that night he'd strangled her and hidden her body in the disused well in the cellar, and told everyone she'd buggered off to follow the soldier. George left the next day on a fast horse he hadn't bought and a short while later, when the stench started to seep up from the well, the villagers discovered why.

When the brothers launched into the account of the spectral coach careening out of the Manor, drawn by the ubiquitous four headless horses (black, of course) and with an equally cranially challenged coachman at the reins, Aidan forced himself to stop listening. It worked until Scott decided to return the favor with a series of wild tales from his journey with Brent Babcock along the Silk Road to Ishkoshim, and the archaeological dig, and soon everyone in the pub was laughing. Everyone except Aidan, and he thanked whatever god looked out for retired agents that Scott didn't blab about the covert mission using the dig as a cover.

"What happened about the book you were taking the photos for?" Aidan asked casually, interrupting a racy anecdote about Babcock and a goat that brought back memories of laughter and sun-hammered trenches.

"The deal fell through. Kind of." Scott's expression was sad but there was a rueful hilarity behind it. "Poor old Brent went swimming off the Barrier Reef and got into an argument with a Great White. He lost."

"Shame. It would have been quite a book. All that hard work you put in—wasted. Not to mention the danger to life and limb," he added pointedly.

"Yeah." Scott heaved a sigh. "Tajikistan isn't the safest place on the planet. But it might still happen. His widow wants me to take his notes and write it myself. I haven't decided yet, but she's in no hurry. Y'know, it wasn't all bad out there. We had some good times," he added, a contemplative smirk growing.

"So here you are in the middle of the English countryside, taking pretty piccies for calendars," Aidan cut in quickly. He could remember some good times as well—the two of them naked in his tent, driving each other to searing orgasms, and trying desperately to stay silent in the process. But it had been a no strings fling and wasn't going to happen again. "Oh, how the mighty have fallen."

"No skin off my nose," Scott said easily. "I got paid for my time and trouble, so it's still money in the bank, though the kudos would have been nice. Who knows, I might just take Candi up on the book deal. Or write one of my own. Did I ever tell you about that temple in South America I was shooting when I spent a month with a tribe of headhunters?"

"Yes!" Aidan groaned and buried his face in his arms.

It was gone ten by the time he admitted a temporary defeat and left Scott to it. When he opened his front door the bloody cat exited as fast as it had entered, and his first step into the living room told him three things.

One, the infernal animal was an un-neutered tom.

Two, it had sprayed up the back of the couch.

Three, the war had escalated to a new level.

\* \* \* \*

No matter what Aidan did, what patented cleaning agent he used, the smell lingered. By morning it permeated the whole cottage and by midday he'd phoned Property Management with an order to replace the damned couch as soon as they could, preferably immediately, and fumigate the place while they were at it. He then retreated to the Red Lion and intended to take up residence there until his home was livable again. Until then, Scott and the memories he evoked had been driven from Aidan's mind. But Scott was there at the bar, chatting with Tom as if they were lifelong friends.

Aidan hadn't expected sympathy, but he didn't expect or appreciate Scott's reaction to his feline-instigated situation. Scott found the whole sorry mess laughable. So much so that by the time Aidan finished telling it, the man was facedown on the bar, practically crying with mirth.

"Damned if I can see what's so funny!" Aidan snapped. "With any luck the scrawny fiend will move in on you next!"

"Not a chance," Scott wheezed. "He likes you. He was only scent-marking his territory—it's what toms do."

"I'll give it 'tom'! I'll castrate it with my bloody boot then we'll see how much scent-marking it can do! And if you don't stop howling like a fucking hyena, you'll be next!"

"A ginger and white job, is it?" Tom asked over the renewed paroxysms of laughter beside him. "Sounds like Mrs Hamilton's Fluffy."

"Fluffy…" Aidan repeated, mildly stunned. Scott fell off his stool.

Luckily, Property Management performed wonders in a matter of hours, and Aidan reclaimed his odor-free home just before midnight.

The following morning saw the next round with That Bloody Cat and Aidan won it by default. He left the house early and via the back door. The animal was lurking on the other side of the road as he limped past his gate and he flipped two fingers in its direction. It glared, sat down, and pointedly washed its well-endowed genitals.

"Yes," he told it. "You take care of them. Push your luck and you can kiss 'em goodbye."

It was a beautiful morning, made sweeter by his victory. The air was fresh and clean and fragrant in his nostrils. Roses and lavenders, dianthuses, and other scented flora were planted with abundance in most of the gardens, along with the ubiquitous honeysuckle.

All in all, Aidan was content, especially as his new neighbor was nowhere in evidence. *Still comatose with any luck*, he mused, though he remembered from past experience Scott was a morning person.

Aidan reached the post office-cum-general store dead on eight-thirty, just as Lucy was opening up for customers. She'd been there since six, as she was every morning, sorting out paper-rounds and delivery boys. She greeted him with her usual smile and they chatted comfortably while Aidan selected bread, milk, eggs, and a couple of packets of his favorite biscuits. As an afterthought he added a packet of best back rashers, acknowledging a sudden craving for a bacon sandwich.

"That friend of yours," Lucy said as she began to ring up his purchases. "Is he—all right?" The slight hesitation implied mental wellbeing rather than physical.

"If you mean Scott, he's more of an acquaintance. And you need to define 'all right'." He shrugged. "He's harmless, more or less. Why?"

"Saw him crawling 'round the Cove first thing this morning," she said.

Aidan's mind supplied the image of the two huge sarsen stones standing at the top of the

271

field behind his cottage, and Scott on all fours. No, couldn't be right. "Crawling?"

"On hands and knees. The sheep were fascinated."

Aidan gave a hoot of laughter. "I'll bet!" he snickered. "He's a professional photographer," he went on, grinning. "He was probably taking shots of them."

"Oh. Arty-farty stuff. Maybe I could get him to do Janey's wedding next month. She still hasn't managed to find anyone at a price she can afford. Is he any good?"

"I've no idea," he said, "but it'll do no harm to ask."

"True. Um, is he married, do you know?"

"No idea. He's always jetting around the world, so who knows? He could have half a dozen wives in as many countries, for all I know." *Or husbands*, he almost added.

"Tajikistan." She nodded knowledgably, ignoring the slander. The gossip grapevine was flourishing in Avebury. "It must have been so exciting."

"Don't believe everything he says," Aidan said. "He's half Irish," he invented happily, "and he didn't so much kiss the Blarney Stone, he bloody well deep-throated it."

Lucy dissolved into giggles. "Mr Whittaker," she managed. "You're awful!"

"Yes," he said, paying his bill. "I am."

# CHAPTER FIVE

Lying on his back in dew-wet grass, Scott contemplated the massive sarsen stone looming over him, stark against the early morning sky. Easily twice his height and almost the same in width, it looked as if it had been there forever, let alone five thousand years. Obdurate. Like Aidan.

Depression settled in Scott's soul. Aidan's defensive wall was as solid as the fucking stone, and wrapped around with vitriol-tipped thorns. He clearly didn't remember Scott with any warmth, and didn't want him around. But maybe it was pain sharpening Aidan's already acerbic vocabulary. Given the gory mess of torn flesh and shattered bone, that he still owned a leg at all was a surgical miracle. Healing from it wouldn't be quick or pain-free. But Aidan was healing. He looked a little better than when Scott saw him a few weeks earlier, and Scott recalled the words of the pub's cook with a wry smile. Ellie had it right. Aidan needed some decent meals under his belt. A lean, mean, fighting machine was great—not to say hot, even. The gaunt look bringing out Ellie's maternal instincts wasn't, and needed to be tackled head on. By Scott.

Which meant he wasn't ready to admit defeat just yet. After all, it was early days in his campaign. He'd give it another try, and a home cooked meal could be the route to take. He cooked three dishes well, and one of them would fit the bill. A visit to one of the supermarkets in Marlborough would get him the ingredients he'd need. Then all he had to do was engineer a conversation so he could slide in the invite to dinner. No, better make it lunch. Less obviously intimate, and Aidan would be more likely to accept. He hoped.

A raven landed on the crest of the sarsen and stared down at him as if wondering if he happened to be a possible snack. Slowly he raised his camera and began to shoot.

\* \* \* \*

Aidan managed to forget both neighbor and cat for some hours, drawn in by the siren call of research, until a burning need for caffeine dug him out of the medieval Persian text.

Wandering back from the kitchen, a strange sound finally caught his attention. It had been there for a while, he realized, a rhythmic, sliding, chinking kind of sound, vaguely familiar and coming now from the front of the cottage. He put down his coffee and peered through the curtains.

That Bloody Cat was tightrope walking

on his fence. And flurries of privet clippings fell like green snow.

Aidan came out of his door like a racehorse from a starting gate, slamming it shut behind him before the furred demon could dodge past him. Except the aforesaid demon didn't bother. It watched the hedge with fierce concentration, ears and whiskers pointing forward, poised and waiting for prey to come hurtling out of the dense foliage. Its tail-tip twitched spasmodically.

Scott Landon, obviously balancing precariously on something, was putting the finishing touches to a now neatly clipped privet barrier somewhat lower than before, thanks to its enforced haircut.

"What the hell are you doing?" Aidan demanded, hands on hips.

"Smartening up our frontage," Scott said brightly, brandishing the hedge clippers. "I noticed it was looking kinda scruffy. Can't have that, can we?"

Briefly Aidan wondered how long it would take to remove Scott's head with those clippers. "There was nothing wrong with the hedge," he snapped. "You do realize you're damaging Omega's property, don't you? They could evict you for this," he added, relishing the thought and conveniently forgetting tenants were supposed to maintain the gardens themselves.

"Oh, come off it," Scott said, grinning infuriatingly. "The fucking was awesome, but we never got the chance to be just friends. So here I am, starting the friendship thing."

Aidan remembered only too well—Scott spread out on the mattress like a pagan god, body gleaming with sweat in the dim light filtering through the canvas, and the scent of sex heavy in the still air. He remembered the lurch of his heart and the desperate need to keep this man in his life for the rest of their lives. And the impossibility of it. Back then his MI6 mission presented a barrier, as well as their age difference. Now he was a crippled ex-agent, and the years between them hadn't changed. Unfortunately, neither had his feelings for Scott. "It was months ago and in a different country, and you were a convenient fuck," he said. "This is now."

"Blah," Scott said, his grin becoming something Aidan could only describe as affectionate, "blah, blah, blah. I'm about to fix myself some lunch. Care to join me? Spanish omelet and salad?"

"Do you really think I can be bribed?" Aidan sneered, ignoring the interested rumble from his stomach.

"By food? Sure, why not? I've got some bottles of Newcastle Brown and Theakston's

Old Peculier chilling."

"Bugger off, Scott!"

"Okay. Come round in half an hour. See you."

"Wait a minute!"

"Lunch. Half an hour. Don't be late. You can't keep an omelet waiting."

Aidan had absolutely no intention of taking up Scott's invitation. No way in hell. His fridge held eggs, bacon, mushrooms, and all the other odds and ends necessary for an omelet of any nationality taking his fancy. And there were half a dozen bottles of Newcastle Brown under the sink.

Admittedly Aidan didn't yet know what the man was doing in Avebury, other than annoying him. He certainly didn't buy the photography story. Calendar shoot? No way. Or the friendship deal. The man was up to something. Had to be. Then it came to him. Scott had branched out into journalism and was planning on writing a piece on ex-MI6 agents. Paranoia reared its head and he didn't rein it in, or he might have followed the urge to give in to the invitation to get to know each other as friends rather than just lovers—except they'd never been lovers—not in the true sense.

Aidan's determination lasted until his own curiosity joined with the savory aroma wafting out of Scott's kitchen window and in through his. They drew him into his back garden, fighting the impulse all the way, and there he found Scott had mutilated the dividing hedge between their respective gardens as well. Still too high to look over, it was now a neatly trimmed green wall. Even his side had been attacked. Scott must have walked all the way round—but no. He'd found another way in. The vandalizing of the hawthorn and rerouting of the roses revealed a tall, narrow, wrought iron gate of uncertain vintage beneath a now shapely arch of greenery close to the cottages. The hinges were glossy with fresh oil.

Vandalism and trespass. Imminent eviction bloomed on Aidan's horizon in a happy, rosy glow. If MI6 wasn't interested in a nosy reporter stalking an ex-agent, Omega could get rid of Scott instead.

"You timed it just right," Scott called. "Come on through, the omelet's on your plate."

Meal first, Aidan decided then he'd phone either MI6 or Property Management and have the bastard thrown out on his ear.

For the second time in a short while Aidan willingly sat down to a meal with Scott. Naturally, it didn't mean he enjoyed Scott's company, and he waited for the opportunity to point it out. He wasn't given one. They ate in the comfortably furnished living room, and in between ingesting a surprisingly excellent omelet complete with chunky salad, warm focaccia bread, and good beer to wash it down, Scott made a couple of feeble attempts at small talk before coming out with what was obviously his main question.

"So you said you were negotiating," Scott said, renewing Aidan's distrust. "Can you tell me what the deal was or will you have to kill me after? I can keep my mouth shut," he added hastily. "Not gonna blab to the press or anything. Even Brent kept you out of his piece in *News USA.*"

"I know. They told me," Aidan said stiffly, his suspicions partially allayed. He hesitated then shrugged. Why not tell him? It was old news in any case. "I'm a deal broker. Or used to be. I was talking with Gulab Turi about forming a cohesive anti-Taliban influence in the area. He was already considering moving against Shaheen Jalil. Babcock's interference brought Mazdak and Shaheen into the open, and the situation came to a boil a lot sooner than planned. Luckily Gulab came out on top. Mazdak, Shaheen, and his son are all dead. Along with two UN soldiers, five Tajik border guards, and fourteen tribesmen."

"Damn. I'm sorry."

"Not your fault. Seven of those deaths I put at Babcock's door. The others would probably have died when Gulab followed the original timetable, and some might say they're down to me and MI6."

"I wouldn't," Scott said quietly. "Regardless of who did the negotiating, Gulab and his Tajik allies made their choice just like Mazdak and Shaheen did, and the region is stable now. There are always consequences." His brief silence was contemplative rather than strained. "Are you going back to archaeology now? You looked like you were having a ball out there when you weren't doing the Secret Squirrel gig."

Aidan shrugged. "Maybe, further on down the line when my leg's as strong as it's likely to get. In the meantime I'm writing articles and taking on freelance translations of old texts."

"Like the Borgia letters." Scott smiled. "And you ended up here. Could you get any farther away from potential hotspots?"

"Probably not. I like it here."

"Yeah. It's very restful. But I gotta tell you, those stones are weird."

Moments later, Aidan found himself discussing the village's unusual setting. Which inevitably led on to photography and reminded him of Lucy's concerns. He started to chuckle and Scott's eyebrows went up.

"Come on," he said. "Share the joke."

"It's no joke." Aidan managed to straighten his face to a scowl. "It's potentially very serious. Not to say criminal."

"What is?"

"Exactly what were you doing on your hands and knees in a field of sheep? The locals do not take kindly to that kind of thing, even if the sheep do."

"And you know about the sheep's preferences because?" Scott's grin was salacious. "I was taking shots of the Cove."

"Arty-farty stuff," Aidan drawled, leaning back in his chair. "Your reputation is already tarnished, you know. And in only twenty-four hours. Not bad going, I have to say."

"Arty-farty?" Scott drew himself up in mock indignation. "I'll have you know I'm damn good at what I do. Art, yes. The fart I'll leave to you."

"Is taking pictures art within the meaning of the word? Art is creating something. Photography is freezing a moment of time."

"And the art is knowing what needs to be frozen, and when and how to freeze it," Scott countered. "Yes, photography is as much an art form as using paints or a sculptor's tools, and I learned from some of the best." He grabbed a couple of books from the shelves behind him, pushed Aidan's plate to one side, and opened them under his nose. "Look at these, and if you deny they're art, I'll shove 'em up your nearest orifice. 'Volcanoes' and 'Streets in the Rain'. Look at the lighting, the composition, the—"

"Okay!" he snapped, pushing the books back at his host. "*They're* artists. Are you? I don't remember seeing the name of Scott Landon attached to any world-shaking photo."

"I do okay." His maddening smirk

caused Aidan to clench his hands around his knife and fork as if the cutlery were twin daggers hungry for combat. But beneath his irritation lay the urge to grab Scott by the ears and haul him in for a devouring kiss.

"Have a look." Scott pounced on the open laptop and his fingers flew over the keys. "I got these with a digital," he went on. "But I mostly use a 35mm. The fancy lenses and filters can't be beaten for serious work, though sometimes I get lucky with the other one."

Aidan stared at the screen. It was set to slideshow mode and four pictures displayed automatically, one after the other.

A vast, gray shape reared against a sky painted in dawn colors of lemon, soft whites, and shades of palest lavender. The harshness of the sarsen stone was shown in minute detail, every pit and hollow, every shadow etched sharp. The photographer must have been lying on his back to take the shot.

Lichen shapes, black, white, and pale yellow, made abstract designs on another stone and formed a similar effect to the Rorschach inkblots. Aidan blinked to stop himself seeing things that weren't there.

Next came a close-up of a sheep's eye, the almost alien shape of the rectangular pupil strangely disturbing—as was the reflection of the standing stones in its blackness.

A close-up of a raven perched on the top of a sarsen followed. The bird glowed in the pale sunlight and its black feathers glimmered like a dark rainbow. It peered down with its head cocked to one side as if it was about to investigate a potential breakfast. There was something very knowing about the cant and the beady, glittering eye focused on the camera. Something very close to menacing. This was, after all, a carrion eater.

"Not bad, I suppose," he said grudgingly.

"Yeah," Scott agreed. "Not bad, but I've done better."

"The Tajikistan shots?" Aidan didn't bother to hold back his snicker.

"Yes, but I took a lot along the Silk Road, and they're not all tied up in Brent's estate. There's an author and his publisher negotiating for them."

"Huh," Aidan said, and reached for his beer.

He didn't stay long after that. Scott was packing cameras and packets of film into a backpack and dropping unsubtle hints about an appointment to meet the farmer with the East Kennet Neolithic long barrow in one of his fields. For a brief moment Aidan expected a casual invitation to go with him to the ancient burial mound, but it didn't come. Instead Scott offered him a smile and a folded piece of paper with an offhand 'see you around'.

It was, Aidan told himself as he went back through the newfound gate, a relief, even though he had a more or less polite refusal waiting to be said. He shoved the slip of paper into his pocket and started to open his back door. As he did so, he caught a glimpse of what might have been a flash of ginger and white in the bushes. It disappeared almost immediately and he scowled. A solid sighting or the figment of an overly suspicious mind? He stepped inside and shut the door. From now on, he'd need to keep a wary eye out for the interloper in his back garden as well as the front.

# CHAPTER SIX

Aidan didn't exactly forget about the slip of paper Scott gave him. He just added it to the small pile of letters sitting in the wire pending tray and made himself a mug of coffee. Then he sat down at his computer, already forgetting his plans to shop Scott to MI6 or Omega. Instead he focused on the Persian text he'd been dragged away from before lunch. Or rather, he tried to focus. For some reason the ancient poetry had lost its appeal.

He glanced at the time readout on the corner of the screen, surprised to see it was nearly two-thirty. He'd spent close to three hours next door, though it hadn't seemed like it at the time. Admittedly, the omelet was of an unexpectedly high standard, and they'd chatted sporadically in easy, companionable drifts between necessary silences. At Aidan's prompting, Scott did his fair share of the talking. The places the man had been weren't as varied as Aidan's MI6 itinerary, but he clearly loved travel as much as photography, and did not hesitate in the face of danger.

Which wasn't enough to explain why Aidan brought up Google and typed in 'Scott Landon photographer' for the first time.

There were a couple of entries matching the man: one a travel book for which he'd supplied the illustrations, the other a new release by Jodi Guildenstern—*Arenas of Conflict*—and an article which not only reviewed the latter, but praised the photographer's skill and predicted a bright future for him. But unfortunately none of the so-lauded pictures were shown.

Scott's talent was undeniable, going by the few photos Aidan had seen, though he would never admit it to Scott's face. A week spent naked in a pit of vipers would be preferable.

Right from the start of his recruitment by MI6, Aidan had accepted involuntary retirement as a distinct probability. So regardless of the alias he took for his work, Aidan Whittaker had slowly and carefully forged a respected niche in the historical and linguistic circles of academia. His life no longer contained the hazards and adrenaline rushes courtesy of MI6. He liked the quiet day to day existence, and became totally and devoutly committed to maintaining it. Scott, he insisted to himself, was an irritating and unwelcome presence in his corner of the world. But even though Aidan found it difficult to accept, he was stupidly glad to see him again. The attraction he still felt and would not, could not, acknowledge, hadn't lessened. Nor, of course, had the age gap between them. Which begged the question, why the hell would Scott be interested in a friendship with a lame, virtually over the hill, middle-aged man? Yet Scott had gone to a lot of effort to find him…

Aidan steeled his incautious heart and turned his mind to Persia. This time the lure of the past drew him in.

* * * *

"Did you know…" said a familiar voice outside Aidan's living room window. It was ajar just enough to let in scented summer air, but not four-legged livestock. "… There are some countries that have more than their fair share of style?" Aidan glared over his shoulder, but no one was leaning in, elbows on sill, to pester him. Nor could he see the speaker. "The Spanish for sure, and Jodi says Italians are hot as well. Now, she's half Hungarian, and if she's anything to go by, Hungarians take a lot of beating. They have real panache. You have the look of a Magyar to me. A Magyar Mog." Aidan rolled his eyes. Scott was talking to That Bloody Cat. "I read the article he did on the language, but there's one very interesting feature he left out."

Aidan pushed the window open and stuck his head and shoulders out. Clematis tangled in his hair, but he ignored it. "What feature?" he demanded.

Scott, leaning down to have an eyeball to eyeball conversation with the cat on the fence, looked up and grinned. "Their profanity shows a strong penile fixation."

"I know!" he snapped. "If I was writing for one of the more lurid tabloid newspapers I'd've made it the central thread! As it is, I write my articles for people whose minds are a little higher than their dicks!"

"It is said," Scott went on, grinning unabashedly, "that your average Hungarian can enter a revolving door behind you and leave it in front. Not many people know that."

"Not many would want to! Don't tell me! Hungary has become the new Tajikistan, right?"

"Has it?" An alarmingly innocent expression crossed Scott's suntanned features.

Aidan ignored it. "Are you fraternizing with That Bloody Cat?" It was a rhetorical question. Of course the idiot was. "Don't encourage it, for God's sake! It's probably got fleas," he added hopefully as the beast rubbed its cheek against Scott's arm. "Anyhow, what do you know about the Hungarian language? Nothing!"

"Right, but I do have a laptop and a search engine. The Alternative Dictionaries site is a revelation, believe me."

"You," Aidan said forcefully, "are no better than That Bloody Cat. Sod off, both of you." He shut the window with a snap and stamped back to his computer. He sounded petty and his cheekbones burned with embarrassment and self-condemnation. Even with the window closed, he could hear Scott's laughter.

\* \* \* \*

Scott shut the door behind him and his amusement immediately died. Lunch had gone well. He'd been on his best behavior, and he hadn't flirted or dropped suggestive hints despite the uncomfortable tightness in his pants. Aidan had gradually relaxed, opened up, and was again the articulate spellbinder with the richly velvet voice Scott had fallen in lust with at the dig. When Aidan finally left, Scott was optimistic. But not for long. *Why? What the hell happened in such a short space of time to reset Aidan to hostile mode?*

It occurred to Scott that maybe he should just give the man some space. His meeting with the East Kennet farmer would only take a few hours. If he extended the trip to a couple of days and went from East Kennet to London, he could kill some time being a tourist. *Aidan might even miss me*, he thought wistfully. *Yeah. Right.*

He shoved toiletries and a few changes of clothing into his backpack, tossed it onto the backseat of his car, and drove off.

Whether or not Aidan missed Scott was a moot point. Scott missed Aidan. He also missed the Magyar Mog, the regulars and beer at the Red Lion, the cozy, old world comforts of his rented cottage. After two days in London, unsettled by the unexpected homesickness, he called Jodi, knowing he could rely on her to jolt him out of it with a slap upside the head—even if it was verbally from Geneva—and discovered she was in Paris. So he bought a ticket for the Eurostar train and she met him at Gard du Nord.

And slapped him upside the head in lieu of a greeting.

Jodi gave him sympathy, a lot of alcohol, and good advice. The chief of which being—once she'd dug the whole sorry tale of his failing Avebury campaign out of him—that he should remember his Shakespeare.

"Hamlet," she said to his blank expression. "Act three, scene two. *The lady doth protest too much.* Think about it." He stared at her and she rolled her eyes. "Good grief, boy! He's trying to drive you away! It's as plain as the nose on your face! Which means you've gotten under his skin."

"Does it?" Scott muttered, depressed again. "Sure as hell don't feel like it. Could be it means he just doesn't care."

"Are you in love with this guy?" Jodi demanded.

"Y-No, I just wanna—I—yeah, I think

maybe I am... Shit, I'm fucked."

"Not yet, Romeo. Would he be resisting you this hard if he didn't give a damn? No. Trust me. So what are you going to do?"

"Go home and carry on?"

"Got it in one."

\* \* \* \*

For several days there was no sign of Aidan's neighbor. The silver BMW was also conspicuous by its absence and he began to hope he was going to be left in peace.

The cat, though, spent its days perched on his front fence, so he continued to use his back door for comings and goings, smugly pleased the four-legged terrorist hadn't cottoned on to the subterfuge. Which, as far as he was concerned, just went to show how false was the assumption of feline intelligence.

However, Scott continued to be an irritant, even in his nonappearance. The staff and regulars at the Red Lion wanted to know where the man was and when would he be back. Ellie-in-the-kitchen became almost maudlin, to Aidan's intense disgust. How the hell could the bloody man have gotten his feet so firmly under the metaphorical tables of Avebury so very quickly? Surely the entire village hadn't fallen under the spell of his superficial charm?

On the third day, Aidan realized TBC wasn't so much haunting his frontage as using his fence as a vantage point to watch his absent neighbor's door.

Damn it, even his archenemy had been seduced.

To test his theory, Aidan opened his front door and walked out, leaving it standing wide behind him. The cat didn't move, didn't even flick an ear in his direction. He limped to the gate. Finally the cat reacted. It gave him a glare Medusa would have envied and carried on with its vigil.

Aidan didn't know whether to rejoice or to feel slighted.

By the fourth day Aidan's reprieve was shown to have been temporary. Lulled into a sense of false security and with an urgent need for more chocolate biscuits, he opened the front door and stepped over the threshold. He was a little slow reaching back to close it behind him and a streak of bi-colored fur was all the warning he got.

"Damn you!" he bellowed, cane thrusting like a sword to bar the way, but the cat was far more swift than any human opponent.

For ten minutes he forgot he was lame and chased the unholy demon around his living room. Papers flew like oversized confetti, books fell, and his computer screen suddenly displayed rows of consonants, numbers, and vowels as flying feline paws tap-danced across the keyboard. His mug and its contents ended up on the floor, spreading a brown stain on the cream carpet.

Finally, having caused as much devastation as a horde of carousing Visigoths, the cat hurtled out the door and Aidan slammed it shut in its wake. Favoring his throbbing leg, he leaned against the frame to catch his breath and surveyed the damage.

The living room was in chaos. He gazed around, stunned. It was almost unbelievable how much havoc one small mammal could cause. Ice grew in his heart and he jerked the door open. The cat was watching 2 Cove Cottages as if nothing had happened.

"You are dead!" he yelled. "I will rip off

your mangy fur with my teeth and nail you up by your boll—"

"Really, Mr Whittaker!" Mrs Hamilton hurried across the road, her champagne-rinsed hair frizzing about her head. She scooped the demon into her arms and it slouched there, smirking at him. "You shouldn't shout at poor Fluffy! He's only sitting on your fence, for heaven's sake! He used to live there until Mr Armitage died!" Her wounded gaze did not pierce his conscience.

"The little monster lives with you now," he said coldly. "If it wants a permanent residence back here, I'll give it one—six feet down!"

"Oh! Mr Whittaker!" She drew herself up, five-foot-two of outraged matronly pensioner, and met him glare for glare. "Fluffy—"

"—is a fiend from the Ninth Circle of

Hades!" he hissed. "Mephistopheles would be a better name! It has wrecked my home, my research, my computer—"

"He's only a cat! Who can't understand why he isn't living with poor Mr Armitage anymore! He wants to come home!"

"Over its own dead body!" And Aidan firmly shut the door on her. To be exact, he slammed it so hard it bounced on its hinges.

By the time he'd restored order and retrieved his on-screen work, Aidan had cooled down. He was uncomfortably aware he'd effectively destroyed any standing he'd gained in the community. By now Mrs Hamilton would have told the tale, suitably embroidered, to her cronies, and they had probably passed it along.

All Aidan could do was apologize to the woman. The thought was galling. She didn't know what kind of Machiavellian creature she harbored and probably wouldn't comprehend if he explained it in one syllable words, with diagrams.

Tomorrow. He'd deal with it then. He'd sealed deals between tribal leaders, talked hostages away from Somali pirates, and arranged prisoner swaps with the Tamils and Sri Lanka. He could do this. Right now, slow and bloody felinicide was the only option he was prepared to consider as far as the cat was concerned.

Aidan's worst fears were realized when he resumed his journey to the shop. Lucy gave him a cold stare and did not offer her usual friendly greeting. She served him with terrifying politeness and turned her back as soon as she handed him his change.

That Bloody Cat had won another round.

## CHAPTER SEVEN

Aidan's cup of tribulations overflowed the next morning. He awoke to a serenade of sorts. The BMW was parked outside, all the windows of the neighboring cottage were open, and a tenor voice was warbling more or less tunefully to an old David Bowie track. Aidan buried his relief under a mountain of irritation. It was a plot. Had to be. Scott was in league with That Bloody Cat to drive him insane. Perhaps he should make that phone call to his old boss, suggesting a certain freelance photographer be repatriated. With extreme prejudice.

No. Aidan gave himself a mental kick. He was made of sterner stuff. He hadn't served Queen and country for nearly one and a half decades in some of the world's more perilous places to be defeated now by the machinations of an American maniac plus a four-legged bag of fur and evil intent.

He had to strike back, or at least attempt to regain some status. He was a highly trained negotiator, for God's sake. If he could keep Ellie-in-the-kitchen on his side, it would counteract some of the damage caused. So at twelve-thirty he set out, limping up Green Street toward the pub.

There was no sign of his *bête noire,* but as Aidan passed the B&B on Green Street, the door opened and Mrs Hamilton rushed out. He braced himself for a fresh torrent of censure, vowing silently he would be humble and penitent, and waited for the first broadside.

But she grabbed his free hand and patted it.

"Don't worry," she said soothingly. "I quite understand, you poor dear, and it was a beautiful gesture, but you shouldn't have bothered. I'm sure they'll write again, soon."

"What?" he began, but she was already bustling back inside.

Aidan shrugged and carried on to the Red Lion with a puzzled frown.

His reception in the pub was... odd. The regulars greeted him with overdone, hearty cheerfulness, not quite meeting his eyes. Ellie stuck her head out of the kitchen and raked him up and down with a critical gaze.

"You don't look too chipper, that's for sure," she said accusingly. "You staying for lunch?"

"Uh, yes. Ham sandw—"

"Steak and mushroom pie," she interrupted, "peas, broccoli, and creamed potatoes. You need a decent meal inside you."

"No, I—" But the kitchen door was already shut.

"No use arguing with her," Tom said,

supplying his pint without being asked. "Pie's got Guinness gravy in it."

"Great, but—"

"It's okay. We all understand," Tom said earnestly, eyes sliding away from Aidan's. "Scott explained."

"*What?*" he whispered. Tom flushed.

"About your leg and the pain. And having the op canceled again. Bloody National Health—"

The rest of the man's words were drowned out by the pounding of rage-driven blood in Aidan's ears. Scott dared to presume— Aidan didn't need his help in anything, and for Scott to use Aidan's injury to garner sympathy was several miles beyond the bounds of his tolerance. What the hell did Landon think Aidan was? A cripple who couldn't fight his own corner? He clutched the bar in a white-knuckled grip to prevent himself from wrapping his hands around Tom's neck in lieu of Scott's. It took a few deep breaths before he could master his fury. Tom didn't notice. He was looking anywhere but Aidan's face.

"Right," Aidan said, forcing calm into his voice. "Fine. I'll just go and sit down, then."

He'd barely settled into his usual place when Scott strolled in. He gave Aidan a fleeting grin, bought a pint from Tom, and after a brief conversation with the barman, he drifted over.

"Mind if I join you?" he asked.

"Yes, I do mind. Fuck off, Landon."

"Thanks." He sat down, stretched his long legs under the table. "You really fucked it up, didn't you?" he went on happily. "But Mrs H is off your back. You owe me for a bunch of roses and an assortment of gourmet cat food."

For a moment Aidan couldn't speak. Then, "You read the Alternative Hungarian site? Good. Try this one for size—*lofasz a valagadba!*"

Scott laughed, the sound rich and mellow. His eyes were sapphire-dark and brimming with delight. "Is that the one about a horse's prick? I wondered how it's pronounced."

Aidan opened his mouth to deliver a scathing and scatological answer, but Ellie arrived with a platter of food. To his startled gaze it looked as if she'd piled on double portions of everything.

"I can't eat all this," he protested.

"You can and you will." Ellie slapped down the knife, fork, and paper napkin. "I've been talking to that Lucy. Chocolate biscuits and coffee, with the odd egg and bit of bacon thrown in for good measure, do not make a proper diet. You don't just need looking after, you need a bloody keeper!" She stalked away, throwing a grim, "There's peach cobbler for dessert," over her shoulder.

Scott stuck his finger in the gravy oozing from the pie and sucked it clean. "Mmm," he purred, eyes closed in lascivious bliss. It was a surprisingly erotic sight and Aidan looked away, fighting his body's response. "Tastes fantastic. Whatever you can't eat, I'll finish up for you."

"Sod off!" Aidan snapped, and started eating.

He cleared the plate, but it was a close run thing. Only because he was too stubborn to let Scott have the leftovers did he manage it. But he drew the line at the peach cobbler. After a short battle of wills between him and Ellie, they compromised on the coffee and she took the dessert away before Scott could acquire it.

Feeling too full to start an argument, Aidan could still muster up some acid. "I thought it was too good to be true," he muttered, sipping his coffee. "The peace and quiet has been wonderful these last few days. But you came back."

"Needed to visit my agent," Scott said with an insouciant shrug. "Then I hopped over to Paris to visit a friend. You should get around more, hit the clubs maybe, have some fun."

Aidan nearly choked. "I'm fine where I am, damn you!"

"Sure you are. It's nobody's business if you want to bury yourself in rural Wiltshire," Scott said with a smile. "I can think of a lot worse places to become a hermit."

"So go and find them," Aidan snarled. "And take photographs."

Scott sniggered and drained his almost full glass of beer in a series of long swallows. Aidan studied his neck, the smooth line of tendons, the movement of his Adam's apple, and wistfully identified where the major blood vessels were closest to the surface. It was a pity Ellie had carried away the cutlery as well as the platter. On the other hand, he could kiss that pulse, feel again the surge of life under his mouth—and he was officially losing his sanity. Friendship was the only reason Scott was being sociable; the man had said it himself. Maybe a sense of gratitude for the rescue as well. Aidan's thigh twinged, threatening to cramp and effectively reminding him of another reason why Scott couldn't be interested in picking up where they'd left off. A wave of bitterness and inadequacy swamped him. He kept it from his expression with difficulty.

"I'm off," Scott said cheerfully. "Have to see a man about a horse." And he left to a chorus of farewells from the rest of the customers.

The BMW was gone when Aidan limped back to his cottage. That Bloody Cat wasn't, though. It perched on its usual place and sneered at him as he passed it. He swung the gate shut with enough force to rock the fence.

In the manner of all felines, the cat turned its fall into a controlled descent and touchdown, and stalked away with its tail upright and twitching in the 'I meant to do that' position.

Hugging the small victory, Aidan went back to his computer and the closing paragraphs of his article on medieval Persian.

Scott either wasn't back the next morning, or he'd returned and disappeared again. At a loose end now the article was finished and sent off, Aidan decided a little gardening would be soothing for his abraded nerves. He wandered out into the back garden with a mug of coffee in one hand and a trowel in the other. The grass was overlong, the weeds in the flowerbeds were taller than the plants, and only the Scott-cropped hedge showed any sign of care.

"Damn," Aidan said aloud and abandoned coffee and trowel on the seat beneath the pergola. He fought his way past the climbing rose and the clematis to investigate the potting shed, rediscovering roses have determined thorns. Sure enough there was a lawn mower in there, an old-fashioned device powered by brute force rather than petrol or electricity. He checked the blades for sharpness, gave it a dousing of oil from the can on the workbench, and hauled it outside.

The lawn wasn't large, but the effort of pushing the mower through the luxuriant grass used muscles he'd forgotten he had, doubly so since he didn't have the full driving power of his right thigh. And the day was becoming progressively hotter. Aidan took off his shirt and used it to mop the sweat from his face, then collapsed on the seat to rest his vociferously complaining leg. Even cold, his coffee was better than nothing, and he drank it, eyes closed, breathing in the lush potency of fresh-mown grass and the scent of the flowers. Birds sang, insects hummed, cats meowed—Aidan opened his eyes.

That Bloody Cat was sitting in the middle of his neatly mown lawn, staring at him with eyes the size and color of newly minted copper coins. Or the fires of the Pit, depending on perspective.

"Bugger off!" Aidan snapped. It struck him he was saying those two words rather a lot lately. He'd have to put his mind to coming up with some alternatives. "I've got a trowel, and I know how to use it. So if you want a grave six feet deep..." The cat lifted a paw, licked it, and swiped behind its ear. Then it hiked up a back leg and began to wash its genitals. "What's the matter? Did you get fed up waiting for your soul mate?" he went on. "He's probably off taking snapshots of horses."

Or maybe he'd finally taken the hint and left. For good. Maybe another, more interesting job had come up. Something dangerous in the Sudan or Lebanon, or somewhere similar. The possibility hadn't occurred to him before, and unaccountably chilled, Aidan sat a little straighter. He'd already learned Scott had a fondness for taking risks. Okay, he didn't want the man in his immediate vicinity, but he certainly didn't want him gone from the world. It would be a dull planet indeed without Scott Landon on it.

Just as Aidan intended to prolong his own life as long as possible, he'd rather like to know Scott was doing the same. Providing it was somewhere else. So Aidan gave himself a metaphorical kick in the arse and forced his concern into the depths of his heart. Then the fine day broke up in an evening thunderstorm which lasted into the night.

He dreamed of explosions and jagged metal.

## CHAPTER EIGHT

Over the next few days, the emptiness of the adjoining cottage, recently seeming a blessing, became something of an ache. He was not worried about the man. Absolutely, positively not worried. Scott was big enough and at twenty-five, surely nearly twenty-six, old enough to look after himself, and God knew he had the devil's own luck. It came to Aidan that perhaps he was missing the verbal fencing, the casual companionship and Scott's easy laughter. And the way the sunlight loved the man's hair, the scent of his cologne, the strength of the young body under his— He hammered the thoughts into oblivion before they could take root.

The Red Lion Regulars continued to treat him with the embarrassed—and embarrassing—consideration the average hale and hearty Englishman usually gave to the physically impaired, and it made him increasingly reluctant to go to the pub. They hadn't been this bad when he'd first arrived in the village, and Aidan guessed the difference was they knew him now. And Scott had probably gone a little over the top on how bad Aidan's condition was when he'd invented the postponed operation. TBC continued to haunt his fence, barely giving him more than a flick of its ears to show it noticed his existence. The day Aidan caught himself selecting a piece of cheese to offer it, was the day he admitted he was perilously close to losing his marbles.

So he ate the cheese himself and decided it was time to give his pending tray some belated attention.

The first thing he picked up was the piece of paper from Scott. On it the man had written the name of the Henge Shop in the High

Street and two titles and authors: *Peruvian Earth Mysteries* by Felipe Hermanes and *Arenas of Conflict* by Jodi Guildenstern. The latter book was one of the two he'd found on Google.

It didn't take the brain of a super sleuth to get the message.

Aidan glanced out of the window. The clematis had taken quite a battering in the storm of a few nights ago, but was fully recovered and seemed to be attempting to turn itself into an exterior screen. Through the filter of green and blue he could see the sun shining in a clear sky. It was about time he took a walk and stretched his legs. He needed to go to the General Store anyhow—he was down to his last Newcastle Brown. That being so, he might as well browse around the Henge Shop afterward.

Ellie was hurrying into the Red Lion as he passed by and she waved to him. "Come for lunch!" she called. "Fresh salmon baked with olives, served with a Greek salad."

He waved back. "Sounds good!" he yelled. And it did. He might let himself be tempted.

As expected, both books were on the shelves of the Henge Shop. The illustrations in the Peruvian one were impressive and atmospheric, moody, titanic walls and idols losing the battle with the living jungle... The contrast of the unyielding stone and the soft fleshiness of the conquering vegetation was striking. Yes, the bloody man had talent, right enough. Aidan put the book back and picked up *Arenas*.

This was markedly different, one woman's account of conflicts in the African continent, and Scott's photographs provided fitting accompaniments to the text. They were gut-wrenching and telling, and part of Aidan stared at the pictures in awe, while another part of him was furious the man might be risking his neck—again—in a high-profile venue when he should be shooting pictures for a bloody calendar. Yet a third part quietly acknowledged these stories needed to be told and one picture was worth a thousand words. It was a cliché, but that didn't mean it was wrong.

Aidan bought the book and took it home.

It was after midnight when Aidan finished *Arenas of Conflict*. He sat for a while in the comfortable armchair by the fireplace and stared sightlessly at the empty hearth, the closed book heavy on his thighs. Photos and text were as compelling as they'd promised to be in his brief page-riffling in the shop. They were disquieting, demanding more than mere attention; they caught the reader by the throat and dragged him into the scene so the death-stench and bitter futility of hate were almost more than flesh and blood could stand. The online review he'd found was right. Scott's talent would take him far.

Aidan stared at the book morosely and considered shredding it. Mrs Hamilton could use it as filling for That Bloody Cat's litter tray. He wished he'd never seen the thing, never knew what depth of expertise Scott Landon revealed, because—

Aidan swore and stood up, found a slight gap on a shelf in his bookcase, and forced *Arenas* into it.

Because even if he came back, Scott would not be staying in this quiet, redolent-with-peace village for a year. It could not hold him. *Aidan* could not hold him. Aidan had absolutely nothing to offer to persuade him to stay. Scott was too vibrant, too restive, too *alive...* The revelation was a Road to Damascus moment and it stole the breath from Aidan's body.

Lightning drew jagged lines across the night sky, flaring its swift light into his room, and Aidan winced. There was no fool like an old fool.

That night he dreamed of horses. White, skeletal horses. They were not comfortable dreams; some might call them ill-omened. They thrust him out of his sleep with Scott's name on his lips, the sound of his voice dull and flat in the lonely darkness.

* * * *

It was an instant of *deja vu*. A car door slammed and brought Aidan out of his chair, his breakfast forgotten. He reached automatically for his cane and dived for the door, jerked it open, and slowed to stroll casually outside. His relief at seeing the silver BMW nearly shattered his usual mask.

"Oh," he said, faux-startled. "You're back. Good. You can take That Bloody Cat off my fence for a start."

"What cat?" Scott gazed around blearily.

Naturally the demon was nowhere in sight. "The one giving a feline imitation of Banquo's ghost!" Aidan snapped. "It's been haunting the place since you went. It's pathetic. Hopefully it'll give me some peace now." He squinted at the unshaven, heavy-eyed human bane in front of him. "Bloody hell, you look rough. What have you been doing?"

"Taking pictures." Scott didn't bother to smother his yawn. "Got some great ones during the thunderstorms."

"Wow, how interesting." Aidan raked his gaze up and down the scruffy and probably odorous body. His clothes looked as if they'd been drenched and allowed to dry in situ. "You look like a train wreck," he said accusingly. "You'd better come in and have some coffee. It'll be hot, at least." And probably stewed, but who the hell cared? He didn't. "Take your boots off outside."

"Yes, Mom." Scott grinned. He muttered something else, the words all but lost in another cavernous yawn.

"For God's sake, hurry up," Aidan said quickly, spotting the feline anarchist loping down the road toward them.

"What the—oh, it's the Magyar! Hey, Mog, did you miss m—"

Aidan grabbed him by a damp shoulder and dragged him inside, shutting the door as the cat hopped up onto the fence. "Stay on the doormat until you've got rid of those mud-collectors you call footwear," he ordered. "I'm not having you tracking God-knows-what across my floor."

He ignored the sniggering repeat of, "Yes, Mom," and marched angrily into the kitchen. By the time he came back with a steaming mug of freshly made strong, sweet coffee, Scott had abandoned hiking boots and socks on the mat, taken over his chair at the dining table and was eyeing up the remnants of his breakfast. Since Aidan had only eaten a couple of mouthfuls of bacon and mushroom, the remains were considerable.

"You," Aidan snarled, "are the living embodiment of a barbarian horde! You're worse than That Bloody Cat! Go on, then, finish it up." But Scott already started in on the sausages, and he moaned what was probably meant to be a 'thank you' around a mouthful. "Seeing a man about a horse, you said."

Scott nodded. "Alton Barnes," he mumbled. "Cherhill, Westbury then Uffington. White horses."

Those kind of horses. Giant figures cut into the chalk bedrock anything up to three hundred years ago. Apart from the Uffington one, which needed another zero on the end.

"There is a school of thought," Aidan said stiffly, "claiming the Uffington horse is a dragon."

"Bullshit. She's a mare." Scott sliced the egg and the yolk oozed out, yellow as buttercups. "Anybody can see that. She is something special."

"Naturally. I take it you did read up on her before you went flying off?"

"Naturally." He mimicked Aidan's snideness perfectly, but softened it with a scapegrace grin. "Any chance of more coffee?"

"Probably," he said, reaching across to acquire a slice of bacon before it was speared on Scott's fork and engulfed. "I thought you were off to another job. Didn't expect you to come back."

Scott sat back from the now empty plate, looking as if he wished he hadn't eaten. "Unfinished business. It's why I'm—" He stood suddenly, a grim set to his mouth. "Thanks for the breakfast. I owe you one."

Aidan leaned against the kitchen doorframe, the cafétière in his hand, and watched him leave, barefoot and with his boots and socks in one hand.

"You're welcome," he said quietly to the closing door.

What the hell was Scott playing at? The conundrum teased at the edges of Aidan's concentration all through the reading of his emails. Not even the request from his editor for a piece on the older Persian poetry traditions could entirely banish it. He didn't think Scott was deliberately playing any kind of game within the strict meaning of the word. But the man had to have a wider purpose for being in Avebury, other than needing a place to stay while he completed the calendar shoot. Surely there was more to it than simply wanting to be friends. Scott as good as admitted it was no accident he was next door. He could rent a place anywhere in the UK to take his calendar photos.

Why here?

It wasn't the first time the question bounced around in his skull. The cliché from Casablanca reared its head and not in a good way. Why *his* village? Despite—or maybe because of—Scott's almost constant attempts at seduction at the archaeological site, they hadn't been what he'd call friends in Tajikistan. Just two people thrown together by circumstance, a mutual dislike of Scott's partner, and an almost irresistible urge to fuck like mink on Viagra. Aidan could see no reason why Scott wanted to form a friendship with him now—unless—

Something tightened in Aidan's belly. Maybe that was it. A lover had died or dumped him and he needed to be around someone who wouldn't give him sickly-sweet sympathy.

Well, Aidan could do that, no problem. He'd invite him for the odd meal, challenge him to darts matches at the Red Lion. Be sociable.

Satisfied he was close to solving the Scott enigma, Aidan turned to research of another kind, and refused to remember the first time he'd given Scott what he'd needed, in the aftermath of Scott's kidnapping by Taliban sympathizers. Scott had needed reassurance he was still alive and safe. After the sexual athletics left Scott sleeping so deeply he might have been drugged, Aidan had held him close, soothed him through the inevitable nightmares, and had realized that like an aging fool he'd fallen in love as swiftly and surely as a boulder falling off a cliff. And hit reality at the bottom. The impact had been bad enough back then. Now it threatened to shatter him.

"It's been great," Scott had said. "Goodbye." Words Aidan knew he would hear again soon enough.

Breathing deeply and evenly, Aidan armored himself against the inevitable. Scott was not and never would be his.

# CHAPTER NINE

Noon, and the weather was too good for him to be sitting indoors. He collected a beer from the kitchen and strolled out into the tranquility of his back garden. The grass had lost the new-mown smell, but the scent of roses more than made up for it. The rambler contesting ownership of the potting shed displayed blooms of deep pink, their heavy perfume intoxicating. The difference a few bouts of rain and sun could have on vegetation never failed to enchant Aidan, and this small piece of real estate was no exception.

Sprawling on the bench, he stretched out his legs, bottle resting comfortably on his belly. Lulled by bee-drone and birdsong, Aidan let his eyes fall closed. Life was good, he told himself. All was well with his world, he insisted silently, and nothing could mar his contentment.

When a questioning *mrouw* broke into his reverie, Aidan raised his eyelids to half-mast and peered around. That Bloody Cat was nowhere in sight. The *mrouw* came again, followed by a chirruping whir, and it emanated from the other side of the hedge. A male voice answered in an indistinguishable mutter, then sighed into silence.

Intrigued, Aidan got to his feet and walked soundlessly to the gate between the two gardens. He could see nothing past the thickness of the hedge, so he carefully eased the gate open. He hadn't paid much attention to his neighbor's garden when he passed through to have an omelet for lunch. Now he gazed around at a lawn and flowerbeds much the same as his own, complete with an apple tree and a potting shed, but no pergola. Instead a white lilac tree provided shade, and lying on the bench beneath it with his head cushioned on a rolled up shirt, was Scott. That Bloody Cat sat on a nearby stump-cum-coffee table, judging by the mug beside the furred bum. The animal gave Aidan the evil eye as he drew nearer, and he paused less than a step away.

Then he forgot his *bête noire* and awareness of his surroundings faded; Scott filled his vision. He must have showered and changed, because the low-slung jeans were not the ones he'd come home in. Other than the jeans, all he wore was suntan and body hair. And small white blossoms drifting down from the branches above to ornament him like flakes of fragrant pearl.

Aidan had always known Scott was handsome. Now he was something more. He slept, one arm resting across his belly, the other trailing down, fingers curled in the grass. His blond hair looked as if it had been toweled but not combed, and it tangled around his face and ears. His lashes lay as if thickened with kohl below the angled curve of his eyebrows, and his slightly parted lips were both vulnerable and sensual in their fullness. It took the shadowing of his beard stubble to nullify the close-to-androgynous aspect of his features.

There was no duality in his body—Scott Landon was a hymn to masculinity—strength and grace lay in every relaxed muscle, every bone and tendon beneath the lightly tanned skin. He was glossy with sweat and the dappled sunlight gleamed on the golden crispness dusting his pectorals.

With medieval Persian still floating around in his head, Aidan smiled. "*Ghulam,*" he whispered under his breath, though this was no youth in Paradise but a man in his prime, poised at the peak of excellence.

A tiny four-petaled flower fell, landing on the corner of Scott's mouth, its touch too light to rouse the sleeper. Instinctively Aidan carefully brushed it away. His fingertips lingered on the pleat of skin, relishing the contrast between silken lip and stubble, the contact surely no heavier than the lilac. But Scott stirred, his head turning on his makeshift pillow toward the interloper, and his sleeping mouth curved slightly in a smile so achingly tender Aidan thought his heart would break. Did Scott know he was there?

With the cool assessment of the mind, Aidan had always known Scott was handsome. Now he knew it in blood and bone and the heavy throb of his pulse. And he hoped suddenly and with a reckless longing that rocked his foundations that he was the sole reason why Scott came to Avebury.

Before he could act on the impulse to wake the sleeper with a kiss and a whispered promise, commonsense came to his rescue.

Slowly and with infinite care, he backed toward the gate, TBC watching him every step of the way. He met the inscrutable copper gaze and the cat yawned, slowly, showing every tooth in its evil head. Then it did what it seemed to do whenever it held Aidan's attention: it stuck a back leg in the air and pointedly washed its balls.

* * * *

Aidan stared at his computer screen and did not see it. The sleeping man beneath the lilac tree filled his thoughts. He'd already acknowledged the depth of his own feelings for Scott, but it was a surprise to imagine Scott might feel the same way about him. The key word being *might.*

But Scott had neither said nor done anything which could be interpreted as a hint he wanted a more meaningful relationship. Just friendship. Of course he hadn't. And if he did, then he certainly wouldn't be looking for it with an academic fourteen years his senior. Aidan was making something out of nothing. Scott hadn't turned toward *him*, per se. He was deeply asleep and sensed the nonthreatening presence of someone he knew. There could be no other reason.

Scowling, Aidan re-examined his original theory. The later chapters of *Arenas of Conflict* featured the latest upsurge of violence in Somalia, so it was not so very long ago Scott and the author risked life and limb researching and illustrating it. And going by her writing, Jodi Guildenstern was as driven as Scott. A good match, then, if Scott swung both ways. And if the relationship had gone down the drain, he could understand why Scott would be looking for a sanctuary of sorts while he got his head and heart back together.

Except he wasn't showing any sign of retreating from a broken affair.

Right now Aidan was the one retreating to regroup. And sooner or later he'd have to assess exactly what kind of game the idiot in the next garden was playing, and what he, Aidan, could do about it.

Later.

Much later.

Irritably, he turned off the computer and stood up, stretching. He needed a stiff drink and cheerful, undemanding company and he'd find both at the pub. He also needed to get away from the distracting mental images, ever-present reminders of Scott's presence. Aidan needed to be at a safe distance.

Ellie was carrying plates of sandwiches to the Brothers Walker when Aidan limped in and sat in his corner with a beer. She detoured toward him on her way back to the kitchen.

"You look like a wet weekend," she said, standing over him with hands on hips. "And you missed the salmon yesterday."

"Sorry," Aidan said with genuine regret. "Something came up, and I couldn't get away." He didn't think it would do much to appease her if he said he'd got his head stuck in a book and lost track of time.

Ellie sniffed. "Leg troubling you again?" More of an accusation than a question, she didn't wait for an answer. "The salmon went like hot cakes and them as missed out asked me to make it again today. So it's on the menu if you're interested."

"I'm interested." He offered her his smile and her expression underwent a grimace of exasperation. "Thanks, Ellie."

"Huh. What about your friend? Is he

likely to show up?"

"No idea. He's back, but that's all I know."

"Huh," she said again. "He's another one who doesn't know what regular mealtimes mean."

"Well, he's got assignments, I suppose," he said with a shrug.

"Yes. Gallivanting about the countryside at all hours and in all weathers frightening the bloody sheep!"

Aidan didn't bother to smother his snigger. "It's a tough job," he said solemnly, "but someone's got to do it."

"Idiots, the pair of you," she said. "My eldest boy is a chiropractor in Swindon. Go and see him. He's good." She fished a business card out of her coverall pocket and slammed it in front of him. "Tell Frank I sent you," she added, and stalked back to her domain.

Aidan pocketed the card and slouched back in his chair. He was trapped in the limbo of waiting for his meal and he could either go chat with Tom or—Aidan sighed and pinched the bridge of his nose. The picture of Scott sleeping half-naked in the patchwork shade wouldn't leave him and from now on, no matter where he might travel in the world, the scents of lilac, roses, or lavender would always invoke it.

He was fooling himself, Aidan decided. Yet when Scott was near, the constant tension between them was—reassuring wasn't the word and neither was comforting—*right* was the nearest thing Aidan could come up with. Which was ridiculous given: a) his own undoubted skill with words, b) he was now an ex-MI6 agent, and c) Scott was a self-confessed nomad.

*All right. Admit you still want the man and decide what you're going to do about it... if anything.* A bout of casual sex might be exactly what Scott needed to get over a broken relationship, just as he'd needed it after the trauma of his capture and rescue in Tajikistan. Aidan could make the offer, and if Scott took him up on it, then they would both get it out of their systems, and...

And that would be the end of it.

Or rather, it would if the other part of this equation wasn't Scott Landon. After all, if sensuality was an Olympic event, the man was a natural gold medalist. No, the unexpected stumbling block was something much greater than mere sexual gratification.

It was the 'C' word, and Aidan was abruptly ambushed.

Until his retirement Aidan was a stranger to it. Commitment was not something he'd ever considered offering anyone when his chosen profession had him disappearing for weeks, months, at a time, risking life and limb—and sanity—whereever MI6 sent him. It was all part of the package deal and he had gone into it knowing the score. But now he had a settled base, a safe harbor, and everything else that went with it, except someone to share it.

Now there was a stubborn idiot who truly believed he could make a difference in the world. Aidan glared at his pint, remembering *Arenas of Conflict*. Could and probably would. If just one person got off their arse and did something because that book and its pictures galvanized them into action, then it was all the justification needed. And Scott would spend the rest of his life traveling the world, having the occasional foray at windmills, championing lost causes, being the eternal optimist, and believing in the ultimate goodness of the human heart.

Aidan gave a snort of sardonic laughter. Poor deluded bastard. But someone had to do it, he acknowledged reluctantly. And that someone would need a haven to come home to, if only for a short time between forays. Somewhere to heal the inner wounds which stayed long after mere flesh repaired itself and, maybe, a shoulder to lean on for a while. And perhaps those fourteen years between them wouldn't matter so much.

Where better than Avebury? Who better than—

"Sod it," Aidan snarled. He was becoming positively maudlin. If that was what Scott was doing to him, he'd better run like hell in the opposite direction before his brain turned entirely to mush and dribbled out of his ears. The bloody man had no business invading his life—Ellie put a platter of food in front of him, and the aroma provided an effective distraction. Even so, he ate slowly, in part to savor the truly excellent meal, but also because Scott would not stay out of his head.

Everything circled back to Scott's

reasons for being here. Aidan still favored the Jodi Guildenstern angle, mainly because he did not want to look too closely into his own irrational impulse.

On the other hand, he'd save himself a lot of heartache if he went back to his original plan and just wrote off the brief episode in Tajikistan as an aberration brought on by too much sun and celibacy, and forget it ever happened.

Confident in his resolve, Aidan returned to his cottage and picked up the thread of his research again. It was unfortunate that a fair amount of the poetry he was studying was homoerotic in nature.

# CHAPTER TEN

He was disturbed by someone knocking on a door. Not his door. It was an insistent bang-bang-bang as if whoever was perpetrating it got more pleasure out of the noise than was decent. Aidan was about to open his window and request a bit of peace and quiet when a woman spoke hurriedly, her voice stressed and urgent.

"Barry, don't do that! Stop it. That's enough. Barry, that's enough! Barry!" The knocking stopped and a child began to howl. Dull thuds sounded, as of small trainers impacting on wood. "Barry!"

"Want to!"

"Barry, you mustn't!" Then the door must have opened. By this time, Aidan was unashamedly eavesdropping. "Oh, um, Mr Landon?" the woman said over the shrieks from the brat. "Um, hi, I'm Jane Elliott—Lucy from the shop's sister?"

"Hi, Jane," came Scott's molasses-slow drawl. "What can I do for you?"

*Now, there was an opening line,* Aidan thought giddily. *Let me count the ways...*

"I, er, don't know if Lucy has said anything to—ow! Barry, stop it!"

"Want to!"

"Lucy told me you're a photographer, and I, um, was wondering if—Barry! Don't kick the flowers!"

"How old is he?" Scott asked politely.

"Four—" she began.

"Nearly five," Barry butted in. "I'm gonna go to school soon and kick things."

"You need to be careful, then," Scott said.

"Don't have to! Why?"

"Because some things kick back. Now try counting up to ten while I talk to your mom."

"Don't want to!"

"Yes, I'm a photographer," Scott continued regardless.

"Well, I'm getting married next month, and we haven't been able to find anyone to take the wedding pictures, and I was wondering if you—ow! Barry, that really hurt! You mustn't kick! Do you do weddings, Mr Landon?"

"I've been known to," Scott said and Aidan could hear the smile in his voice. "Call me Scott, please. When is it?" The brat was unaccountably silent.

"The twenty-seventh, here at St. James's church."

"What's that?" Barry demanded.

"A stone," Scott answered. "It's very old and magical."

"I want it."

"Can't have it."

"I'll kick you!"

"Then you certainly can't have the other magic stone I've got indoors. The twenty-seventh should be fine, Jane. Tell you what, give me your address and I'll come by this evening. We can talk about what pictures you want then, and how many, okay?"

"Want the stone!"

"Hey, Barry, I'll make a deal with you. If your mom tells me you've been good from now until I call, I'll give you this magic stone. Deal?"

"Deal."

"No kicking and no shouting?"

"Yeah."

Jane's sigh of relief was clearly audible, even through the closed window. "That's great, Scott. Thank you—but I, um, we can't afford much."

"Hey, we can sort something out," Scott chuckled. "Barry, quit it."

"It's a cat."

"Yes, and he won't like it if you grab—"
There was a screech of feline outrage and an
equally piercing yowl from the child.

"Sorry about that," Scott said, sounding
not at all regretful.

"No, no, it's his own fault," Jane said
wearily. Barry's howls were enough to rattle the
windows. "It's only a scratch on his hand. I
suppose it's the best way for kids to learn."

"Tough on the cats, though. I'll come by
at about seven?"

"Great. I'll try to get Barry into bed by
then. Thanks a lot, Mr Lan—Scott."

"You're welcome."

The sounds of juvenile lamentations
gradually lessened as Barry was led away, but
Scott didn't go back inside. Instead he obviously
decided the wounded dignity of That Bloody
Cat needed sympathetic attention. "Poor old
warrior," he crooned. "You gave the little

monster a good'un, though."

Aidan opened his window and leaned out. "Magic stone?" he drawled. By the look of him, Scott had just come in from the garden. He was still sleep-tousled and shirtless, and looked good enough to eat. No wonder Jane had been tongue-tied. That Bloody Cat was cradled in his arms, its tail lashing angrily. It flattened its ears at Aidan, a low growl grating in its throat.

"A piece of flint with a crystalline flaw. Found it at Westbury." He held it up and rolled it around his fingers like a stage magician, somehow without dropping the cat in the process. "It's good for distracting kids."

"Oh. Is it okay?"

"What?"

"It. That Bloody Cat."

"Oh, sure. Just lost a bit of fur and some dignity. Don't suppose you've got some milk I could borrow, have you? I meant to go to the store but I dozed off."

"I should think so. Come on in, but leave that outside."

"Do I have to?" Scott all but pouted. "He is housetrained."

"Stop whining. You sound like the little horror." Scott sighed and put the cat down. It immediately began an intense grooming session, apparently designed to remove all taint of miniature Homo sapiens from its fur. "You're a fool for encouraging it," Aidan went on as he opened the door to let Scott in. Thankfully, the cat was too busy to attempt an entry.

"I like him. He's got character."

"Not the word I'd choose to describe it."

"You should give him a chance, he really likes you."

"Bullshit. It is a fiend from Hades. So you're going into the wedding trade now?"

"Thought I may as well. Did you see

her? She's a pretty girl, though if the poisonous dwarf's going to be there, her day could well be ruined. Got a face like a pug. Which is a good thing for a pug but unfortunate for a human." Scott must have thought he'd said enough, because his mouth clamped shut and he shoved his hands into his pockets.

"I took a look at those books you recommended," Aidan said into the slightly awkward silence. "They're not bad." Then, "Jodi Guildenstern can certainly write."

Scott's face brightened. "Yeah, can she ever. Jodi's Pulitzer Prize material. About four years ago she did one on the Chechen rebellions and before that, she wrote an incredible book on the Serbo-Croat conflicts. This one's better."

There was no reluctance to mention her name, just a warm pride in a friend's success.

"Is she likely to drop in to say hi?" he asked casually.

"Hell, no." Scott chuckled. "She's on promotional tours at the moment, advertising the book and trying to get the UN moving. It's like pushing an elephant uphill on a greased slope. But she likes taking on the big guys. I've done my bit with the pictures."

"So what's your next project going to be?"

"After the calendar and Jane's wedding? Thought I'd take a look at North Korea."

"Shit." Aidan stared at him in consternation. "You're mad," he said. "Do you have a death wish?"

"No. I've got this ambition to find out what it's like to be a hundred years old..."

"And you'll manage that by taking happy holiday snaps in North-bloody-Korea?" Aidan demanded indignantly, and spoke again before he thought. "I'd like to be there with you, celebrating your century, but if you're planning on hitting all the major trouble spots on the planet, there isn't a snowball-in-hell's chance of you being alive for it to happen!"

"Would you?" Scott asked, voice quiet and expressionless.

"Would I what?"

"Be there, with me?"

Everything locked down. Aidan's throat, his lungs, his heart, and he could only stare, slack-jawed. Was Scott saying what he thought he was saying?

"Just kidding," Scott said quickly, too quickly, and laughed.

Pain and anger struck through Aidan. "Not in a million years," he snarled. "Clear off."

Scott left. Without the milk.

Aidan slumped into the nearest armchair and dug the heels of his palms into his eye sockets. He replayed the scene in his head: Scott's      sudden      defensiveness,      the uncharacteristically clumsy attempt at humor, and the lack of response to his summary eviction.

What if he meant what Aidan thought— hoped—he meant? "Shit," he whispered, his stomach knotting. "Shitshitshit."

He sat there for a long time, unmoving, until instinct told him it was nearing seven o'clock. Then he stood up, a grim set to his mouth, and stalked to the door. He jerked it open just as Scott left his cottage and opened the gate.

"I'll make a deal with you," Aidan said, voice as controlled as he could make it. "If you want, I'll be there on the condition you come to Avebury after North Korea, and after every other deathtrap you walk into." *Come back to me no matter where you go in the world.* But he couldn't say it aloud. "Deal?"

"Deal," Scott said gruffly, turned on his

heel and carried on up Green Street.

Aidan watched until he was out of sight then closed the door. To discover That Bloody Cat had strolled in and made itself at home. It sat in front of the empty fireplace with its paws tucked away, resembling a furry tea cozy. But there was nothing relaxed about it. Its tail was a loose curve on the rug, the tip twitching.

"Clear—" he started, but stopped abruptly. He'd said it to Scott, words he'd call back if he could, make it so they'd never been spoken between them.

Somehow Aidan needed to find a way to regain their common ground. Because although Scott had agreed to the deal, it didn't mean he'd heard the subtext. Restless and unsettled, Aidan poured himself a large brandy, picked up his cane and the C.J. Cherryh paperback he'd been planning on rereading, and took them out to his garden. He left the back door ajar, so his invader could leave on its own terms. This once.

## CHAPTER ELEVEN

Dusk came slowly, intensifying the perfume of the flowers. TBC loped out of the cottage and disappeared through the hedge, to terrorize the local wildlife, Aidan surmised. He thought he ought to get off his arse and see if the demon had sprayed his furniture again, but he was too comfortable lounging beneath the pergola.

There wasn't enough light for him to read by now and he closed the book with a sigh. The sound of movement next door brought him back to the present and he sat up, reaching for his walking stick. It was probably only Scott coming home, but Aidan never assumed anything when it came to possibly unwelcome visitors.

A light came on next door and it flooded out into the garden as the back door opened.

"Hi, Magyar," Scott said, and a *mrouw* answered him. Aidan relaxed and let his cane drop back against the bench. It made only a small noise, but suddenly Scott was silhouetted in the gate-arch.

"Aidan?" he said. He sounded wary and that hurt. "Have you got a minute? About the deal we made. Can we discuss the small print?"

Something tightened under Aidan's breastbone. It occurred to him it might be hope. He came smoothly to his feet and walked to the gate. "Sure," he said and opened it, stepping back to swing it wide and gesture Scott across the threshold. Silent as a shadow, Scott moved past him. Aidan left the gate open, giving him an avenue of retreat, just in case. "The small print?" he prompted.

"Yeah. It's your deal, so what's in it?"

"Whatever you want there to be," Aidan said with as much casualness as he could scrape together.

"Will you stop playing word games!" Scott snapped.

"All right." Aidan decided to take a chance. One swift step forward brought him chest to chest with Scott; then he tilted his head a little to one side to avoid an embarrassing nose clash, and kissed him.

He'd intended it to be just a kiss. A chaste suggestion as to what could be on offer if Scott wanted more. Instead all his barriers were breached by a surge of complex emotions so intense he could not retain a rational thought, and Scott responded with wholehearted enthusiasm. Aidan deepened the kiss and their tongues met. Then he was searching, tasting, relearning the contours of Scott's mouth. Scott's arms were around him, pressing him so close he could feel the leaping thuds of the man's heartbeat. Or maybe it was his own and they were in sync.

In sync. Yes. Just as they were meant to be, he realized dizzily, welcoming the hands burrowing under his shirt to find skin. He did some seeking of his own and was rewarded by the smooth glide of muscles under his palms as Scott tightened his embrace. He hadn't been held with such strength and confidence in a long time. Too long. His blood was flowing fast and free through his veins, and he felt more alive with Scott in his arms than he had for months. Since Tajikistan. But Aidan needed answers to a few questions. He braced his hands against Scott's chest and held him at arm's length.

"What you see is what you get. A semi-crippled academic many years older than you, and I'm not in the market for a short-term fling. If you and I get together, I want long-term. Commitment. If it's not what you want, leave now."

"No way am I leaving!" Scott insisted heatedly. "You're the—"

"Why did you come to Avebury?" Aidan interrupted.

"For you," Scott said as Aidan hoped he would. "I was going to take it slow, kind of ease into your life…"

"And now?"

"Am I there yet? In your life? Because you're the one I want in mine. You want commitment, you got it. Good enough for you, you stubborn, autocratic asshole?" Somehow the insults sounded like endearments.

Aidan believed him. "Yes," he answered and began to laugh in quiet exultation.

"What?" Scott demanded, lips beginning to work on the side of his throat.

"Come to bed."

Scott followed Aidan into the cottage

and up the winding stair, too aware of Aidan to take much notice of his surroundings. Aidan managed the stairs okay, his limp hardly in evidence, Scott observed. He wondered about the actual damage to bone, muscles, and ligaments, and what it would mean to Aidan in the years ahead. Aidan didn't seem to have much in the way of hang-ups about his wound, and Scott couldn't see him letting his lameness get in the way of anything he wanted to do. He himself didn't know enough about such injuries and their aftermath, but he could find out. And if there were things he could do, like help with Physio Therapy and massage, he'd take the necessary courses and learn how. Then they were in Aidan's bedroom, and suddenly Scott was as nervous as a virgin, hesitating in the doorway.

Aidan switched on the light and crossed the room to draw the curtains across windows looking out over the road and the back garden respectively. He paused halfway between Scott and the bed, a wry smile growing.

"Cold feet?" he said. "We don't have to do this."

"The hell we don't." Scott's confidence came back in a rush and he strode forward. Aidan didn't back away and they met in the middle of the room, the bed only a few feet from them. "I thought you were dead!" he said with quiet intensity. "Do you have any idea what it was like? This great gaping hole opened up in my life and all I could think was I lost someone so important and I never knew how important until you were gone! So, yeah. We have to do this."

Slowly, carefully, half expecting Aidan to call a halt even now, Scott edged closer and slid his arms around his waist. But Aidan didn't pull away. He settled into the embrace with a sigh, and his smile no longer showed its wry twist.

"Idiot," Aidan murmured.

"But you love me, right?"

"Yes, I'm rather afraid I do."

"Damn, could you sound any more British?"

"Probably. If I put my mind to it."

Scott threw back his head and laughed. "God," he said. "I love you—don't ever change!"

They undressed slowly, taking their time. The night stretched before them, all the nights and days they could wish for. Scott took a long, slow look at Aidan's body, and not only with a lover's eyes. Aidan finally stood before him, naked, his cock semi-erect, his jaw set in something like a challenge, giving Scott his opportunity to check him over. Aidan's leanness was borderline skinny, but that would change as he clawed his way back to fitness. The scarring on his right thigh wasn't as bad as Scott expected. The pucker of the exit wound and the thin lines left by surgery still looked red. They'd fade in time. The slight muscle atrophy would disappear with steady exercise.

"Well?" Aidan demanded, hands on hips. "Want to check my hooves? My teeth? I'm sound in wind if not in limb, I assure you."

"So I should hope." Scott smiled. "Yeah, if you were a horse, I'd buy you, Doc." He touched the narrow wing of silver hair at Aidan's temple. "You're looking good," he said honestly. "I missed you. Have I told you?"

"Come here," Aidan whispered and opened his arms. Scott walked into the embrace and buried his face in the man's neck. Emotion threatened to choke him, stung in his eyes, but he fought it down. Aidan was warm and alive and naked—and his. Aidan must have sensed something, because he rubbed soothing circles on Scott's back for a short while. Then he stroked down his spine to cup his buttocks and pull him in, sandwiching their cocks side by side between their bellies.

Successfully distracted, Scott arched with a groan of pleasure. "Yesss!" he hissed and sought one of those deep, gently voracious kisses Aidan was so good at giving.

Scott lost all track of time and place. Everything narrowed down to Aidan and the sweet glide of their bodies as they rocked together. He barely registered the bed that miraculously appeared beneath him, lost in the joy of Aidan's weight pinning him, Aidan's hands firing sparks of sensation wherever they touched.

"Want you in me," Scott croaked, "and for God's sake, don't tell me to be quiet! The walls are about six freakin' feet thick!"

"Two." Aidan chuckled. "I have something that'll do for lube. Do you have condoms?"

"Pants pocket."

"Okay. Stay there."

"Hah!" Scott snorted. "Do you really think I'm getting off this bed until I absolutely have to?" While Aidan rummaged in Scott's discarded pants, Scott searched the drawer and cupboard in the bedside table for the promised lube. All he found was a large pump dispenser with a prescription label on it. "This?"

"Yes. It's moisturizer for my scar tissue. We'll get the real deal tomorrow."

"Great. In an industrial-sized bottle."

"Optimist."

"You bet! I'll buy you Viagra if you think you'll need it."

"Is that why you have a strip of six in

your pocket?" Aidan asked, waving the foil packets at him.

"Maybe." Scott grinned. "We'll stock up on them as well."

Laughing quietly, Aidan came back to the bed and stretched out beside him. "I missed you, too," he confided, and kissed him before he could frame a coherent answer. "Kneeling isn't easy yet, so—"

"I can bottom from the top," Scott interrupted eagerly.

"Or we lie on our sides."

"That, too, but tonight I want to see your face when you come."

"Likewise." Aidan kissed him again, tongue licking possessively deep. No one kissed quite like Aidan, Scott decided, though of course he could be biased. Scott welcomed him in and started an oral exploration of his own.

Once more time and place drifted away

from Scott, leaving him swimming in a sea of pleasure. Just like the first time in the tent, Aidan was making love to him, his body moving with Scott's, lithe and sure, in a steady climb toward ecstasy. When Scott thought he was done for, climax a breath away, Aidan gentled him down.

"Easy," Aidan murmured, as if Scott was a horse fighting the bit. "Don't want you coming yet. Wait until I'm inside you."

"God! Did you have to say that?" He drew in a deep, shuddering breath, struggling to keep control. Sweat gleamed on Aidan's skin, highlighting the long curves of his muscles as he reached for the cream dispenser, and inspired Scott to drag his tongue across the nearest part of Aidan's anatomy. "Mmm. You taste good." He dropped his head back on the pillow, carding his fingers through Aidan's hair.

"And you feel good. Think you can hold

out?"

"Oh, yeah."

Aidan squirted a quantity of the white salve on his fingers, and Scott didn't need to be told to open his legs. He also took a firm hold on his own cock, tightening his fingers around the base in an attempt to stave off premature ejaculation as Aidan's clever fingers stretched and prepared him. Those fingers weren't enough; he needed Aidan's cock in him with a hunger bordering on desperation. "If you keep on doin' that, Ah'm gonna—"

"No, you're not." Aidan rolled onto his back and placed an unwrapped condom in Scott's hands. "Come on, lover, your turn to do some work."

"Lover." Scott grinned like a fool. "I like it. Can I call you honey?"

"No. Get on with it."

Laughing his delight, Scott propped

himself on one elbow, leaned down, and kissed him. "Baby," he whispered. "Sweetheart. Darlin'—"

"Idiot." Aidan laughed with him, but stopped on a gasp of pleasure when Scott took his cock in hand and pumped it slowly.

"You were sayin'?" Scott drawled, and wished he could tease for a long time, get a little loving payback. But he was too hungry, and going by the pre-come slicking his hand, so was Aidan. Quickly Scott rolled the condom onto Aidan, gave it its own anointing of the makeshift lube, and settled himself astride the man's hips. He reached back and guided the cock's blunt head to the entrance to his body, locked his gaze with Aidan's, and slowly sank down.

The sensation of heavy fullness nearly overwhelmed him. He hadn't experienced anything like it for months, not since he stopped hooking up with men who resembled a certain dark-haired Brit, and even then, they'd been a poor substitute. Aidan stroked Scott's cheek and he turned his face into it, kissed Aidan's palm before rising on his knees and lowering again.

"Yes," Aidan said on a groan. "Do it." He trailed a line of delicious fire down Scott's chest and belly, took his cock and balls into his grasp, and gently worked them. "Ride me, lover."

Scott needed no more encouragement. Leaning down, he captured Aidan's willing mouth in an eager kiss, then set up a driving rhythm he wouldn't be able to keep to for long. All too soon the gathering, tingling rush began, drawing up from his limbs to center on his groin. Even as he convulsed in orgasm, Aidan shouted his name, hips jerking under Scott's weight, and Scott began to laugh in exultant delight. He collapsed to one side, not yet in enough command of his limbs to do anything about cleaning them up.

"No stamina." Aidan shook his head dolefully. "And here I was wondering when you'll be in a fit state to screw me."

"Soon," Scott promised, peering heavy-eyed as Aidan removed the condom and rooted in the bedside drawer for tissues to clean up with. "Very soon. Just gimme a minute..." Aidan chuckled and rolled them together.

"Super-stud," he drawled, and pressed a kiss to Scott's brow.

Ten minutes later, Scott was on the verge of sleep.

"You know," Aidan said drowsily, "you were bloody lucky to get the cottage next door." The silence stretched and he squinted down at the blond head resting on his chest. "Is there something you want to tell me?" he demanded ominously, though his fingers continued to walk gentle paths up and down Scott's spine.

"Mrs Hamilton," he murmured, pausing to flick his tongue over Aidan's right nipple. "She introduced me to Maggie Trimm, and Maggie recommended me to Omega."

"You sneaky bastard!" Aidan growled. It didn't come out as forcefully as he would have liked, because Scott chose that moment to add a hint of teeth to the tender suckling he was currently inflicting on Aidan's breast.

"I wanted to be close to you," Scott said, coming up for air. "I still do. I want us to be together for a very long time, and a very wise woman told me we should get to know each other, be friends as well as lovers. Do you want that, too?"

"Yes," Aidan whispered huskily. "She's right. We need to take it one step at a time."

"Agreed. So we'll keep the gate between

our back yards well-oiled, yeah?"

"Yes."

Scott chuckled. "Great. You are the most important person in my life and you always will be." He raised his head, his mouth sensual and swollen. His eyes were blue as the sky at twilight and fathomless. "You always have been, from the moment I saw you, only I was too dumb to realize. Do you think Omega would sell us both cottages?"

"What?" Aidan managed, breathless.

"So we can get a connecting door knocked through inside. We can't keep on using the hedge gate. Especially in winter."

"Now that is a definite possibility." But, "When were you planning on going to North Korea?" he asked.

"North—? Never heard of it," Scott answered, and kissed him with gentle voraciousness. There was completion in the kiss, joy and desire and a sense of coming home, a profound and abiding love, and Aidan knew he would never be alone while this man lived.

\* \* \* \*

A new day and a new beginning. Heavy-eyed and weary, his smirk feeling as if it could become a permanent fixture, Aidan opened his back door and stretched. He ached a little in interesting places and he didn't need to check in a mirror to know there was a necklace of love-bites along both collarbones. They would fade swiftly enough, but in every important way they would always be there. He'd put similar brands on Scott's more than willing body last night and this morning. Aidan chuckled quietly. Then his gaze focused on the pergola and the book on the bench. He could see the dew glistening on the cover. His cane lay there as well, both of them silently accusing him of gross negligence.

"Damn," he said and started forward. And froze. His bare foot rested on something small and cold and cushiony. It didn't move. Luckily his full weight hadn't come down on the thing and it took only a second for him to identify the object. He jumped back, cannoning into Scott, who immediately wrapped both arms around his waist and nuzzled his neck.

For once Aidan barely noticed. In front of him on the doormat were two bodies—rats on their backs with pink paws in the air, and That Bloody Cat came sauntering up as if it owned the sodding world.

"Aaaw," Scott sighed idiotically. "He's brought you a present! I told you he likes you."

## THE END

# ALSO BY CHRIS QUINTON

Available at **Silver Publishing**:
*Starfall*
*Game On, Game Over*

THE FITZWARREN INHERITANCE
*The Psychic's Tale*
*The Soldier's Tale* by RJ Scott
*The Lord's Tale* by Sue Brown

Available at **All Romance Ebooks**:
*Dark Waters*

Available at **Manifold Press**:
*Sea Change*
*Aloes*

FOOL'S ODYSSEY TRILOGY
*Fool's Errand*
*Fool's Oath*

Available at **Torquere Press**:
*Breaking Point*
*Clue Game*

**As Chris Power**

Available at **All Romance Ebooks**:
*Argent Dreaming*

**with Terri Beckett**

*Tribute Trail*
*War Trail*
*Nettleflower*

CPSIA information can be obtained at www.ICGtesting.com
Printed in the USA
BVOW071347260613

324351BV00001B/123/P

9 781614 953647